Came as 'Me' Left as 'We'

21 stories to escape with

Alfie Dog Fiction

Printed in the United Kingdom

First Printing, 2013 Alfie Dog Limited

The author can be found at: authors@alfiedog.com

Cover image: Elisanth

ISBN 978-0-9569659-9-8

Published by
Alfie Dog Limited
Rose Bank, Norton Lindsey,
Warwickshire, CV35 8JQ
Tel: 07712 647754

CONTENTS

INTRODUCTION

Alfie Dog Fiction has over 1,000 stories available for download. This collection of 21 stories brings together authors from Europe, Australasia and North America in a unique blend of writing for our readers to enjoy. Many of the authors have other stories on the Alfie Dog Fiction website so if you have enjoyed these then we hope you will enjoy the others too.

Both our readers and authors cover many countries. Therefore, it is our policy not to standardise spellings but to leave them to reflect the voice of the author, after all, who's to say we would be right on the spelling we chose? It is part of the fascinating challenge of reading to open a window onto how language has changed through separated usage.

We hope that you will enjoy this selection as much as we have.

www.alfiedog.com

1

CAME AS 'ME' AND LEFT AS 'WE'
Caroline Scott Collins

Helen had returned to the resort keeping a promise she and her husband had made to themselves a few years ago. She didn't think she would want to go because she knew memories and ghosts would be waiting there for her, but it was friendly and familiar and she figured a person staying alone would soon start chatting with other guests and with long-term staff members.

The informal atmosphere of the daytime changed in the restaurant in the evening; black and white uniforms and bow ties for the waiters replaced the brightly coloured Caribbean style open-necked shirts worn during the daytime. A table d'hôte menu and waiter service replaced the self-service buffet and increased the air of formality. Helen mustered up the courage to ask for a table for one. The headwaiter led her to a table set for two.

She sat down and began anxiously staring out of the unglazed window, grateful the shutter was propped open to let in the gentle, refreshing sea breeze. Watching the waves lapping on the shore, just a few feet away, gave her something to do to avoid looking at the empty seat opposite her. In her peripheral vision she could see a shadowy image of John sitting there, looking tanned, relaxed and happy. She sighed.

Dean, the waiter, approached and greeted her warmly. 'Hello, welcome back.' He shook her hand.

'Hello Dean, how are you?'

'I'm good and you?'

'I'm good thanks.'

'On your own?'

'My husband died.'

'I'm so sorry,' said Dean, 'but I'm glad you came again to visit your friends.'

'Thank you. I've been made very welcome.'

'What would you like to drink?'

'Sparkling wine, please.'

'Of course, I'll bring it to you.'

Dean turned and left and Debbie the waitress came and took her food order. Debbie was new—polite, but aloof.

Helen waited quietly, staring out at the waves watching them lap gently onto the white sandy shore under the dark, starry sky. She avoided looking at the vacant emptiness in front of her; nothing felt lonelier than the unoccupied chair—it made her miss John more.

'Oh this is daft,' she silently reprimanded herself, 'you can't sit staring out of the window all night.' Dean returned and removed the cutlery and glasses from the place setting. Another waiter removed the chair to add to another table for a large group of guests nearby.

'Thank you,' she said, smiling gratefully.

'You're welcome,' replied Dean, carefully placing her glass of wine on the table. He left to deliver more drinks orders and she spread out her things to fill the table space, so it didn't look so ominous, and opened the book she was reading on her iPad. Propping it up in a comfortable position, she began to read.

She gulped her wine rather hurriedly at first; Dean passed by with the bottle and topped up her glass.

Sometimes she glanced up from her reading to look out of the window or to peck at her food as it arrived; the view of the canopy of stars and the gentle plopping waves, and eating her meal slowly distracted her—anything to avoid looking at the tables around her, occupied by couples and groups chattering together. The wine began to take effect giving her a fuzzy warm feeling, which helped her to relax.

When the coffee arrived Helen noticed the restaurant was quieter. She was so absorbed in her book she hadn't realised her fellow guests had departed. The music drifted in from the bar outside, the entertainment had begun. Now, feeling a wine-induced haziness and replete from her meal, she felt less self-conscious about sitting alone. The unoccupied tables seemed less intimidating. She sighed to herself thinking 'that's another ordeal over.' She slowly sipped her coffee and returned to her reading.

When she had finished her coffee, and she noted that the waiters anxiously fluttered about her laying the tables for breakfast, she felt compelled to leave. She gathered up her belongings and put them into her bag, drained the last dregs from the wine glass and stood up. 'Next challenge!' she muttered, as she pushed the chair under the table and headed for the exit.

The crowded bar with people dancing and the musicians playing gave her something to do again. She wandered up to a vacant stool near the bar. 'Is anyone sitting here?' she asked the lady sitting on the stool next to it.

'No, that's fine. Join us,' she said, 'the more, the merrier.'

Dean, who was now serving behind the bar, presented her with another glass of wine and grinned as she said 'thank you.' Helen stayed with the group for a while, making small talk about the resort and watching the entertainment. She enjoyed their company and had another drink with them before retreating to the solitude of her room.

The next lunchtime, Helen decided to walk up the path to the cliff top shack for lunch. She figured there would be a nice refreshing breeze up there to cool the heat of the sparkling sunshine. She knew that seeing the wooden scrap John had etched with *"Helen and John, Clatterbridge, UK, 2002, 2004, 2005, 2007, 2009"* would make her heart ache, but once viewed and the memories recalled of happy past holidays she could lay that ghost to rest.

She wandered up the steps and the steep concrete path, past the cliff top pergola where there was a wedding going on. A few guests gathered together in the shady, white-painted shelter, decorated with garlands of flowers. The bride and groom looked blissfully happy.

She thought of herself and John on their wedding day. 'I hope you live happy lives together like John and I did,' she whispered and turned to continue her stroll up the path. Two mongooses gambolled across the path in front of her, darting in and out of the bushes which jolted her back to the present. She rounded the bend and glimpsed the brightly coloured Out House perched on the cliff top.

Helen wandered up to it and under the shade of the corrugated iron roof extension with its adornments of 'souvenirs'; scraps of wood, flip-flops, sarongs, swimwear or underwear, or just local stones with messages scrawled on with a marker pen. Some of the messages were cryptic and meant something special to those who visited; others were just sweet and inspired a story that probably bore no relation to the original meaning.

A little old lady called Celestine had been running the charming ethnic eatery for years and she greeted everyone as a long lost friend. She rushed forward to hug Helen. 'Hello,' she said, 'You come back! You not been a lo-ng time. Youz alone?'

Helen hugged her back, 'Yes, John died.'

'Oh Iz sorry,' said Celestine, 'he's with de angels.' And she hugged Helen again in consolation.

'Youz having lunch?' Celestine asked.

'Yes please,' replied Helen.

'You know how dis works; take a beer and I ring de bell when de food is ready,' smiled Celestine.

'Thank you,' said Helen. She turned to take a beer from the icebox and removed the crown top with the bottle opener, secured to a wooden post with a piece of string nearby, and descended a few gravelly steps to sit in the partial shade of the trees looking out over the bay in the direction of Devil's Bridge. She glanced around at the various souvenirs nailed up all over the place reading them; some made her smile. Then she settled herself at a table and looked out across the turquoise-blue bay, lost in thought.

A voice snapped her from her reverie. 'Goodness me! It's Helen Lather!'

Helen looked round to see who had spoken and saw a vaguely familiar face, but she couldn't think from where. 'Do I know you?'

'You should,' he replied, 'we were at school together. Tim Shadbrook.'

'Good grief, so it is. Tiny Tim!'

'I've not been called that for a few years!'

'Well, I've not been Helen Lather for a few years either.' Helen laughed. 'Are you staying here?'

'Yes, arrived today. Love this place—it brings back happy memories. Haven't been for a few years. Can I join you?'

'Sure.' Helen gestured at the bench seat opposite her. 'Well Tiny Tim, you don't quite suit your name any more; you must have had a late growth spurt. How are you? What have you been up to?'

'Can we make it Tim, please? In my fifties I'm a bit old to be Tiny Tim!'

'Okay, Tim. So what have you been doing?'

'I travel the world as a freelance photographer and I do a bit of writing. I come here every so often to chill out.'

'Hmm, I know what you mean. We've been here several times.'

'We? Oh sorry, I didn't mean to intrude.'

'No, it's okay, I'm here on my own, John died. Anyway, what about you? Are you married?'

'Nah, never got round to it. Truth is I missed my chance when I was fifteen.'

'Crikey. That was a bit young to give up!'

'Broke my heart she did; she never noticed me.'

'Who did?'

'You did.'

'Me? I don't remember—we never really knew each other at school.'

'No we didn't—but I always hoped... I adored you from afar with your blond hair and blue eyes. You always smiled and were so kind to everyone.'

Helen blushed. 'Why did you never ask me for a date then?'

'Too shy. Anyway, you only had eyes for Rod Bellinger in the sixth form. You never gave any of us boys in our year a chance.'

'Gosh, Rod Bellinger—I'd forgotten about him! He didn't even notice me.'

'Ah well, then you know how I felt.' Tim's brown eyes looked sad.

'Yes, but it didn't scar me for life. I married John Sutton when I was twenty three.'

'Ah, John Sutton. He went off to university didn't he?'

'Yes, he became a university lecturer eventually. History.'

'Ah, and I opted for a life of a camera, rucksack and sandals. I dropped out and went travelling.'

'I bet you've been to some nice places?'

'Oh, yes – white sandy beaches fringed with palm trees, exotic temples in the middle of nowhere, and mountain plateaus that make you feel as though you are on the top of the world. I've been really lucky and taken some pretty nice photos to sell, to feed my addiction.'

'Addiction?'

'For travel.'

'Oh I can understand that. John and I had some wonderful holidays...' Her voice trailed away and she paused, and then continued quietly, 'now I'm adjusting to travelling on my own. It feels weird.'

The lunch bell rang.

'Would you like another beer?' asked Tim.

'Yes please.'

Helen and Tim wandered slowly up the rough steps and joined the short queue for the buffet, picking up salads before selecting jerk chicken, ribs and hot dogs from the barbecue.

'Let me take your plate,' offered Helen, 'if you're getting the beers.'

Helen took the plates back to their table and Tim

joined her with two beers, which in the heat quickly gathered condensation on the icy-cold glass. They tucked into their meals.

'Do you have children?' asked Tim.

'Yes, two – boy and girl. Nick's a session player for a music studio in London and Lucy works for a big advertising company. They've bought a nice flat together and look after each other. I don't see them very often – they're busy. Sometimes they pop home and sometimes I go and stay with them, when I want to visit *the big smoke*.' She smiled weakly.

'And what do you do?' asked Tim.

'Nothing much,' Helen shrugged, 'my whole life has been John and the kids—and now I'm on my own, so I guess I need to find something to do.' Helen sighed.

'I'm sorry; I didn't mean to make you sad. So how did you find this place?' Tim's cheery smile emphasized the dimples on his cheeks and his eyes twinkled brightly again.

'Recommended by friends and we've been several times. There's our plaque there,' she vaguely pointed in the general direction. 'Have you done one?'

'Sure, it's around the corner in there, on a blue flip flop.'

'Just the one? Not a pair hung neatly together?'

'Yes, just one.'

'When I see a single flip flop without a partner I always wonder what happened to it.'

'I haven't the slightest idea. I found mine washed up on the beach, so it kind of presented itself for recycling.'

'Celestine's is a good place to display it and give it a new lease of life—as a piece of artwork,' Helen grinned.

'How long are you staying?'

'Three weeks. I just want to chill and think about my future.'

'I'm chilling too, I want to take some photographs and visit my aunt here. I'm going to hire a car; do you fancy a trip out over the island with me? Lunch in St John's perhaps?'

'Are you asking me on a date?'

'Sure. I'm a little less shy now and there's no Rod Bellinger around. I think after about forty years I should at least ask, I might get lucky!' Tim grinned cheekily again.

She smiled at him, 'That would be lovely, thank you.'

They gathered up their empty plates and bottles and placed them on the washing-up pile and put the bottles into an empty crate.

'Thank you, Celestine,' called Helen, who was deep in conversation with another 'old friend'.

'You're welcome. Come back again.'

'Sure will! Bye.'

Tim and Helen started sauntering back down the path and once again the mongooses darted around the scrubby bushes at the side of the path.

'Your aunt lives here, in Antigua?' asked Helen.

'Yes, she lives with my cousin now. She's eighty and a bit frail. My family doesn't get together much anymore; the Atlantic is a big place to cross when you are getting old.' Tim hesitated and then continued, 'If I had asked you out when we were at school, would you have gone on a date with me?'

'Probably, but I would have got into all kinds of trouble with my parents. They didn't approve of mixed race relationships; me going on a date with a black guy would have pushed their tolerance somewhat. But who's to say? We might not have liked each other and one date would have been it.'

'I'm glad I've waited all these years and I bumped into you again. I probably would have got into trouble with my parents too—then,' Tim conceded. 'Attitudes have changed.'

They reached the pergola still adorned with flowers, but now bereft of wedding guests. They walked over and stood in its shade admiring the view. 'My aunt lives in a little house in the village, over there, past the phone mast.' Tim nodded in the direction. 'We used to come to this beach when I was a little boy. My dad would play football with me, and me and my sister would splash around in the sea. Afterwards he'd buy us ice creams at the restaurant at the far end of the bay that's now derelict and closed up.'

'How lovely! So how come your family abandoned paradise to live in cold, wet and miserable England?'

'For a better life. My dad got a job; he couldn't find work here and we got an education. So life was okay.'

Helen looked at Tim. He was taller than her with a slim firm body, and handsome with shiny ebony skin and sparkling brown eyes. And those dimples—'Why didn't I notice you at school…?' she thought. She smiled at him.

Tim took her hand in his and led her back to the path. She glanced back up the path in the direction of the Out House and spied a mongoose scurrying across and disappear in the long grass. She thought she also saw a shadowy figure of John too, smiling at her and nodding; he turned as if to walk up the path and his apparition faded in the bright sunlight. 'John approves,' she thought.

'Come on,' said Tim, 'I think we have a bit of catching up to do!'

'We do, and I think it's going to be fun.' Helen smiled.

2
SWEPT AWAY
Patsy Collins

Jamie ran along the coastal path ahead of Hilary.

"You not coming, Mum?" He called.

"There's someone else, down there," Hilary said. She knew she should have stayed away.

Jamie came back to her. Together they looked down at the beach. A man, and a boy about Jamie's age, were at the water's edge writing words in the sand and watching the tide erase them.

"But it's not their beach; it's ours," Jamie said.

The beach wasn't Hilary's though she'd once felt it was.

Eight years ago when she and Jamie's father were on honeymoon it seemed their own private place. They'd written words of love in the sand and kissed until the tide came in. She guessed the tide had swept away the words before they'd got back to the hotel. That didn't matter; their love would last longer. It had; but not long enough. She didn't like to calculate how soon Tony's marriage vows had been swept away by the redheaded girl in the accounts department where he worked. Hilary had been so lonely since then; no one seemed to understand how she felt.

She wouldn't have returned to the beach except she'd won a week away for a family of four in a competition advertised in the local paper. She'd hoped for a runner up prize of a half day in a health spa. She rang the organisers to say she wasn't a family of four. Half an hour later they called back.

"You can still take the holiday. We're going to contact the runners up and if any of them are in the same situation we'll offer them your unused half of the prize. I imagine single parents are even more in need of a break than bigger families are."

"That's true," she'd agreed. Hilary did feel in need of a break away and Jamie would love a holiday by the sea. She accepted her prize.

Yesterday it had been cold and the beach was deserted. Jamie had been so happy running about after his kite, throwing a Frisbee and skimming stones. Hilary had enjoyed herself too. She thought she'd made the right decision in coming here. That was before she'd seen a man writing in the sand.

"Mum?" Jamie looked worried and she realised she'd been paying more attention to the past than to him.

"What love?"

"Is it their beach?"

"No, anyone can go there."

"Come on, then." He ran ahead again.

Jamie tried to fly his kite, but it was difficult. The wind wasn't as strong as on the previous day and both he and Hilary were unable to ignore the man and boy who continued their game of writing words and watching them disappear. They laughed together as the sea washed away the letters.

Jamie's kite dropped down near the couple. He ran to retrieve it, then stood near them and called to Hilary.

"What are they doing, Mum?"

The other boy answered. "Making nasty things go away."

"How?" Jamie asked.

Hilary came close to Jamie. "Come on, love; leave them in peace." She held her hand to him and said sorry to the man.

"No problem," he smiled.

Hilary thought she recognised him. He frowned at her as though he too was trying to decide if he'd seen her before.

"I know you, I think?" he asked. "Did I see your picture in the paper?"

"I won a trip here, so you may have done."

Hilary remembered now; his picture had been next to hers as he'd been awarded half her prize.

"Then thank you," he said and offered his hand.

Hilary shook it and introduced herself and Jamie.

"I'm Mike and this is Danny."

"So how do you make bad things disappear?" Jamie asked.

"Easy," Mike said. "What don't you like?"

"Broccoli."

"Go on then, Dad," Danny urged.

Mike wrote the word in the sand, then they all stood back and watched the sea sweep it away. The boys both cheered.

"Anything else?" Danny asked.

"Mum crying," Jamie said.

"Jamie!" Hilary felt her face flush.

Mike wrote 'crying' and they watched it vanish.

"I've already done loneliness," Mike confessed.

"And it's gone?"

"For the rest of the week at least?" Mike asked. He gave a hopeful smile.

"I suppose this beach is big enough for four of us,"

Hilary said.

She had done the right thing in coming back.

3
SIGNWRITING
Angela K Blackburn

'We need something modern, but elegant,' said Claire, stuffing yet another custard cream into her mouth.

'Yes, I agree. But I'm not using the word 'services'. 'It makes us sound like we don't know what we're doing,' said Gemma, leaning back in her chair and looking pensive.

Nodding Claire said, 'how about, cleaning, housekeeping and catering, with the business name and contact number underneath.'

'Yes, that sounds good, I think I'll do some sketches later, show you them tomorrow, see what you think.'

'Good idea,' Claire replied, 'who are you going to use to do the actual signwriting?'

'There's a new chap advertising in the local paper, Dad said they'd used him at work and he was very good, so I'll try him first.'

Early the following day they had half an hour before they were due at their first appointment so grabbed a coffee and began discussing Gemma's sketches.

'I like this one in yellow; it'll look great against the blue of the van, stand out really well. The figure of the cleaning lady looks like you,' Claire joked.

'Oh thanks. But what about this one with the pictures of food and drink?'

'No offence, but I think it looks too cluttered, you can't

really tell what it is either.'

'No, I guess you're right. Simple is best. I'll give the signwriting chap a ring and see if we can pop over later.'

Their busy day passed quickly and by the time four o'clock came around, they were tired, hungry and dirty, but excited about the prospect of a professionally sign written van.

Following the proprietor of 'John Soanes – Signwriting' into the workshop, both girls raised their eyebrows in admiration of the fine figure of a man walking in front of them. Claire pretended to swoon then both of them tried to giggle quietly. He offered the girls guest seats opposite his desk which was covered in computers and printers.

'As I mentioned to you on the phone, I've done some preliminary drawings that we both like and wondered if they could go on both sides of the van?'

'Can't see that being a problem. Let's have a look.'

Folding out her piece of A3 paper, John gave a low whistle,'Very nice, sure you don't want to come and work for me as an artist instead of a cleaner? These are really good.'

Gemma laughed, 'Thanks, but no thanks, I'll stick with housekeeping.'

'OK, then, let's see what we've got on the computer by way of ladies with mops. If there's nothing suitable, I can scan in your drawing and use it.'

After an hour of deliberating, they all agreed on the final design.

Claire felt her eyes glaze over as she watched John hard at work. He was gorgeous. She began wondering if he was seeing anyone, married even? She clocked the third finger of his left hand and felt Gemma kick her ankle. Her head flicked round in her direction,

'Sorry, did you say something?'

'I asked you what you thought of the final design,' said Gemma.

John had turned the computer monitor round to face the girls, the final design was on screen.

'Oh wow, yeah that looks great, very professional, thank you John.'

'No problem,' he replied. 'Just need to book you in for the installation, when would be convenient, bearing in mind it will take a couple of hours to do? I need to clean and prime the surface before applying the lettering.'

'Oh right,' Gemma said. 'How about Friday afternoon. I've got a dentist's appointment anyway, so Claire could drop me off, then bring the van straight here. How does that sound?'

'Fine with me,' Claire replied.

'Great. Have booked you in for Friday afternoon, see you then,' John replied.

Waving goodbye they jumped back in the van.

'Cor, he was rather scrummy,' Claire said, excited. Glad I'm the one coming back on Friday. I could look at him all day.'

'Claire! I thought you had a faraway look in your eye earlier. He was rather cute though.'

As the week wore on Claire became more and more excited about a return visit to 'John Soanes – Signwriting'. She had googled his website and sat swooning over his picture.

'Do you think he's married?' she asked Gemma one day.

'Who?' Gemma snapped as she was tackling a particularly nasty blocked sink.

'John. John Soanes, the sign writer chap.'

'Probably,' replied Gemma.

'I didn't see a ring on his finger.'

'Well maybe he doesn't wear one for work, some men don't. Now could you please come and give me a hand, instead of dreaming.'

Friday came and Claire was so excited at the prospect of seeing John that afternoon that she was hardly getting any work done and driving Gemma round the bend. Thoughts going through her head were of candlelit dinners, champagne, late night walks on promenades and picnics on sunny afternoons, not mops and dusters.

'I never thought I would be pleased to say I had a dentist's appointment.'

Claire dropped Gemma off at the dentist's, and then made her way through the increasing Friday afternoon traffic. She'd touched up her makeup for the umpteenth time, hoping she didn't smell of bleach too much. John greeted her with a warm beaming smile and she swapped van keys for a steaming coffee mug. Leaning against the wall she watched John as he got to work. His long, lean body was tanned, a rich horse chestnut colour, his soft curly hair was tousled from working; oh how she'd love to run her fingers through it. What was he saying?

'Sorry, pardon?' she said.

'I asked if you enjoyed your job?'

'Yes, it's great. We get to work when we like and keep all the money for ourselves, a bit like you really. You been doing this long?'

'Couple of years. Worked for a firm on the industrial estate next to the city centre and got fed up with the commute, so decided to set up on my own. Haven't looked back.'

'We aren't doing too bad either, getting more and more

customers every week. We do cherry pick a bit more now though. When we first started we took anyone on.' Claire stopped talking, realising she was babbling, she had a tendency to do that when she was nervous. Watching him work was fascinating she found. He cleaned the side of the van with some sort of strong cleaner, 'it was to get the best possible stick,' he told her. Applying one letter at a time and then lastly the image was time consuming work.

'You have to make sure it's straight, otherwise it looks ridiculous.'

Claire laughed, 'Yes I suppose it would.' Her heart beat increased every time he spoke to her. Could this be the real thing? Love, finally? She checked his wedding ring finger again. Nothing, not even a mark. Her smile brightened.

Looking round the van after he'd finished, she admired his work, the neatness, the accuracy, the attention to small details; it looked very professional, just the image they were wanting to portray. Gemma would be pleased.

'How's it look?'

'Excellent, you've done a great job, thank you very much.'

'Another satisfied customer,' he said.

Passing him her now empty coffee mug, his hand caught hers, they both looked down at their hands touching, then feeling embarrassed both drew away at the same time. The mug fell to the floor, crashed on impact with the concrete and smashed into twenty pieces.

'Oh, I'm so sorry,' Claire said, her hand flying up to cover her mouth after a sharp intake of breath. 'Let me replace it, I'll go and buy you another one immediately.'

'Please, don't worry about it, it's just a mug, I've got

plenty of others.'

'I'm really sorry. At least let me clear it up, I'll just fetch my dustpan and brush.'

She dashed round to the back of the van, collected her tools and set to work clearing up the shattered pottery.

'Where should I dump this?' she asked, showing him her full dustpan.

'Oh, just put it in the bin over by the door, and thank you, you didn't have to do that.'

'It was the least I could do, I'm sorry.'

'Please, forget about it.'

Dumping the shattered mug, she followed him into the office. He sat behind his large metal desk, making the whole place look and feel very masculine. Passing her an envelope, he said.

'Your bill, I'm afraid.'

Claire laughed, 'Oh yes, I'll pass this onto Gemma, she'll sort that out.'

He stood and walked her through the workshop, back to the now very professional looking van. Opening the door for her, she settled herself into the driver's seat and he closed it behind her. She flicked the switch for the electric window and beamed at him.

'Well thank you very much indeed again, it looks great and sorry about the …'

He cut her off by putting up a hand in front of him, as if to say 'enough said.'

Driving out of the workshop, because she couldn't find another reason to stay, she gave him her biggest smile and drove off. Smiling and squirming with excitement she managed to stay accident free all the way to Gemma's house.

'Come and look at the van, it looks fab,' Claire said to a

groaning, head in hands, Gemma.

'Oh wow, he's done a really good job, very professional.'

'He was,' Claire replied, gazing at the sky. 'You OK?'

'Filling,' Gemma replied, pointing to her mouth.

'Oh, poor you, can I get you anything?'

Gemma shook her head. Pulling the envelope out of her back pocket, Claire offered it to Gemma.

'It's the bill,' said Claire, Gemma groaned again.

The following lunchtime Claire nipped into a greetings card shop, whilst Gemma sat eating her sandwiches in the van. After much deliberation she purchased a good 'builder's tea' sized mug, on the front was written, 'Sorry,' in big red letters.

'What you got there?' Gemma asked.

'Oh a replacement mug for John. If I drop you off first this evening, I'll take it straight round to him.'

Claire arrived at the workshop just in time to see John packing up for the day.

'Oh, Hello, to what do I owe this pleasure?' he asked.

Claire smiled and giggled, 'I bought you a replacement mug,' she replied, offering it to him. He unwrapped it and laughed at the wording,

'You didn't have to do that.'

Claire shrugged and looked at her shoes.

'Say, I don't suppose…' he started.

Claire looked into his big blue eyes, saying a silent prayer.

'I don't suppose you'd care to have a drink with me this evening would you?'

'I'd love to.'

'Great. Say eight o'clock at The Grapes wine bar?'

'Yes, OK, I'll see you there.'

'Look forward to it. Thanks again for the mug,' he smiled.

Halfway home Claire couldn't control her excitement any longer and let out a loud 'Yes,' whilst pumping her fist into the air. Texting Gemma later, she asked her what she should wear. Gemma's text came back saying, 'Something smart but comfy'. 'Very helpful,' Claire muttered to herself.

She decided on her black and white striped dress, slightly sixties in style, with a wool shrug and black pumps. Styling her hair and carefully applying her makeup, she wondered about John. She knew next to nothing about him. How old he was. His family background. Did he have any kids? So many men did these days.

She arrived at the wine bar, ten minutes early and went straight inside. The place was packed, mainly her own age, all drinking, laughing; glad the working week was over. She spotted John in a crowd of people over the other side of the bar and pushed her way through the throng. He caught her eye and winked, walking round his friends to meet her.

'Hi,' he said, kissing her lightly on the cheek. 'What can I get you to drink?'

Claire smiled, 'Red wine please.'

He pushed through to the bar and came back with two large glasses of red.

'Let's go outside, see if we can find a table in the courtyard.'

She followed him out into a pretty courtyard, filled with pots, overflowing with trailing plants and flowers and vines climbing up trellis.

'How lovely,' Claire said as they sat on a bench in one

corner.

'Yes, I like it here. They serve lovely wine and good food too. Thanks for coming this evening. You look lovely.'

Claire blushed, unused to the attention and managed a shy, 'Thank you,' in reply.

Chatting amiably about work, life and anything at all, Claire relaxed, enjoying John's company. One glass of wine led to another, then another; tongues loosened they were soon laughing and joking like they'd known each other for years.

It began to get dark and looking at his watch, John said,

'Blimey, its ten past eleven, I must go, sorry.'

And with that, he went, leaving Claire sitting with a half empty glass of wine in her hand and a shocked expression on her face. The barman who was collecting glasses, asked,

'Miss, Miss,' touching her arm, 'you OK?'

'Yes, I think so. My date has just left, rather suddenly.'

'Shall I call you a taxi?'

'Yes, please.'

Riding home in the back of the taxi, she re-lived the evening. They seemed to be getting along just fine, she hadn't said anything to upset him or annoy him, or she couldn't recall doing. Her mother was still up when she entered the house.

'Hi, Claire love, did you have a good evening?'

'Yes, thank you Mum. Off to bed now. See you in the morning,' she called from the bottom of the stairs, not wanting to face her Mother's Spanish inquisition.

Gemma called round the following morning.

'Well? How did it go?'

She told her the full story, including the abrupt end.

'I imagined him walking me home, hand in hand, kissing on the back doorstep. Instead he just left, before I even had a chance to say goodbye.'

'Oh, I'm sorry, Claire, I know how much you were looking forward to it,' she said, dragging her friend into a hug.

Days and then weeks went by, Claire didn't hear from or see John at all. Unbeknown to Gemma she sometimes drove past his workshop on her way home, but the place was always locked up with no-one around.

Their business got busier, new clients were coming along every day, so she threw herself into her work, her Friday evening with john becoming a distant memory. She sometimes worried that he'd tried to get in touch with her, but couldn't, all he had was the works mobile number, but Gemma didn't mention if a call had come through for her.

Two months passed. Tuesday morning's appointment was to clean the local community centre. They were on a tight schedule; it was being used at ten thirty for a funeral wake. Working extra hard and at lightning speed they finished just in time as the caterers were coming in. Sitting in the van sipping hot welcome coffee, they relaxed, not due at their next appointment for an hour. A large black BMW drove into the car park and out from the driver's door, stepped a rather solemn looking John, dressed in a black suit and tie. Claire coughed out her coffee all over the dashboard.

'Claire!'

'It's John, look,' pointing to the BMW. In a flash she was out of the van and running across the shingled car park. 'Hello, John.'

He stopped and looked in her direction, a sombre smile spreading across his face. Claire stopped a few metres short of him, noting his paled expression and red rimmed eyes.

'Oh, Claire. Hello, how are you?'

'I'm fine, how are you?'

'Not very good. Look I'm really sorry for running out on you the other week. I can't stop to explain right now, this is my Mother's wake, the rest of the guests will be here soon. Will you meet me in the wine bar again this evening? Please?'

Claire scuffed at the gravel with her toe and said, 'OK.' Turning, she walked back to the van and then remembering her manners turned around and said, 'Sorry for your loss.'

Getting back in the van Claire told Gemma what had just been said. Gemma asked, 'Are you going to meet him?'

'I don't know, what if he doesn't turn up?'

Later that day Claire ran the conversation over in her head. Part of her felt sorry for John, losing a parent was never easy. But the other part of her was angry at him for leaving her stranded that evening. She decided to go, give him the benefit of the doubt and to get an explanation.

Entering the wine bar this time was completely different, there were only a few tables occupied, one by John. He'd got changed. His jeans were clean and his open necked shirt revealing a few chest hairs was neatly ironed. He saw her come in, smiled and rose to greet her.

'Thank you for coming. I didn't know whether you would. What would you like to drink?'

'Just a tonic water please,' she replied.

She sat at his table and watched him at the bar. He

looked sad, she hoped everything had gone well today, or as well as could be expected.

'First let me apologise to you for running out on you, it was unforgiveable and second let me explain why. My mother raised me alone, my father walked out when I was a baby, never wanted to know I even existed. She was a strong woman, fiercely independent, a woman of her own means. I idolised her, she was always there for me, but brought me up to know my own mind. Then she was diagnosed with cancer, it was a terrible blow. Her medication controlled it expertly in the beginning, but as the disease progressed the effectiveness wore off.'

Claire let him talk, explain, not interrupting, just holding his hand in hers.

'Towards the end she liked me to be home to give her, her final medication of the day and a kiss goodnight, we never knew if it would be her last.'

Claire had tears in her eyes, had she not seen him that morning, she wondered if she would have believed him.

'I'm so sorry, Claire, running out on you like that was unforgiveable, but I didn't feel I could explain all that to you on our first date.'

'Oh John, I'm so sorry, she sounded like a wonderful woman, she was very lucky to have you.' She turned in her seat to face him more, took hold of his other hand and said,

'Of course I forgive you, how could I not?' Her thoughts then turned back to candlelit dinners, champagne and romance as she looked into his big, baby blue eyes and he into hers, believing in him through his pain, looking forward to a hopeful future together.

4
MOVING ON
Jan Baynham

Winter had arrived with a vengeance that year. It was another bleak, December day and it reflected Claire's mood. A solid stone weighed heavy inside her chest. Every morning when she opened her eyes, she felt a black emptiness and even a disappointment that she had woken up at all. A profound dread that she was going to have to make it through the day would envelop her; since she had returned to live near her home town a year ago, she had been having more and more of these grey days.

'Why don't you leave my head? You're always in there. Go away! I can't stand it any more,' she said out loud to James. He wouldn't hear. He was almost two hundred miles away. Their acrimonious break up had affected her more than she admitted even to herself. London had been too full of memories and a very lonely place to live once she was on her own. She hauled herself out of bed and made her way downstairs.

'What's the point of having a big house like this if I've got no one to share it with?' she thought, feeling sorry for herself. Half of the proceeds from the sale of the flat had enabled her to buy a solid black and white semi high above the Bristol Channel. It backed onto a lane lined with trees, leading down a steep path, through the wide open space of parkland and eventually to a grey pebbly beach. She *had* thought she would be happy living here.

Not long after she had moved in, Claire had got herself a black and white English sheepdog whom she'd named Smithy.

'That'll help you settle,' her mother had said. 'There's nothing like a dog for company. He won't let you down.'

He was her companion now, but even Smithy's unconditional love was not enough to lift her feeling of utter wretchedness. The only good thing was that Smithy needed exercise, and long walks down to the park and along the beach meant that Claire had to go out of the house.

'Come on, boy,' she said. 'I suppose we'd better face the day.'

Smithy ran around the kitchen in circles and barked in approval.

Claire gasped as she took her first breath of the frosty, clear air and blew onto her mittened hands. At least she was fully awake now. As they made their way down the lane, Smithy seemed to head in the direction of the beach in a very determined manner so different from his usual meandering and sniffing of the plants and trees on the way. In fact, Claire had a job to keep up with him.

"Hey, wait for me, Smithy!" she called. "We're not on a marathon, you know."

But Smithy was way out in front. The dog was making for a wooden hut which was set among the trees on the very edge of the park where the grass and beach pebbles met. It was only when she got near that Claire even noticed it. The wood was in dire need of painting and the two steps up to the door were overgrown with weeds and brambles. The only sign of habitation was the curl of grey smoke which emitted from a rusty pipe of a chimney. Smithy began barking at the closed door and Claire realised why as she got closer. She could hear the distinctive playing of a violin coming from inside the hut. Smithy had obviously been able to hear the high notes of the violin almost as soon as they'd started down the lane, but they'd only become clear to her human ears at a much closer distance.

The door opened and a swarthy good-looking young man came out 'Hey, what's all the fuss about, boy?' he said. 'Don't you like my fiddle playing?' Smithy kept on barking and wagging his tail until Claire had arrived to put him back on his lead.

'I'm sorry if my dog disturbed you,' she said to the young man. His appearance suggested that he had slept rough last night; his hair was dishevelled and his face showed at least one day's growth of dark stubble. Through the door of the hut, she could see the warm glow of embers in a brazier at the far end of the room.

'No worries,' the young man beamed. 'It's good to see another friendly face down here. I'm Barnabus Hopkins but please call me Barney. I'm a travelling musician and I'm staying here for a few weeks.'

'Hi, pleased to meet you, Barney. My name's Claire Thomas. I walk my dog here most days, but haven't seen you down here before. I must say you can't half play that violin. I'm a musician too – I play the flute but not as well as you can play that fiddle.'

'You look frozen, Claire. Do you want to come in and have a warm? Come and tell me all about your flute playing and the kind of music you like.' Barney opened the door wide and Claire and Smithy entered the wooden hut.

Claire could not believe what she was doing; she had never met the man before but there was something about his warm brown eyes that assured her he was genuine and it was safe to go in. For the first time in months, Claire realised she had forgotten about her troubles. In fact she hadn't thought about James since she'd left the house, not once. Without realising it, she was soon enjoying what Barney was telling her about his nomadic life. It was so different to her structured life as a solicitor in the City and her life now. She'd never taken any risks; everything had been planned out, school, university, career. Even her life with James had become so predictable and, she hated to admit it even to herself, *boring*. But here she was, sitting in this derelict hut listening to a man whom she'd never met before, fascinated and full of admiration for someone who took life as it came.

Barney spent his days down on 'The Island', as the locals called the seaside area, playing his fiddle and busking for any coins that people would give him. The cold winter weather meant that the visitors were few and far between; he would be moving on soon.

'I'd better go and do some work,' he grinned. 'Call in any time you're down, Claire. I could do with some adult company, especially an attractive young lady like yourself.'

Claire found herself blushing. She couldn't believe how much she had enjoyed talking to Barney and knew she would be walking Smithy down to the beach again tomorrow... and the next day.

Every morning before Barney left for his day playing his fiddle on the sea front and every evening after he returned, Claire and Smithy could be found down by the beach where strains of the violin and the flute could be heard complementing each other while Barney and his new friend played traditional folk songs together. Smithy had never had so many walks in his life. It became a ritual that Barney would have the coffee and breakfast ready for the arrival of Claire and Smithy before he left for work and she would have a meal ready for him on his return from busking.

'I've never had company each morning for breakfast like this before,' said Barney, patting Smithy who was wagging his tail in agreement. 'Even better that the company likes making music with me too!'

He winked at Claire. She reddened but beamed back at him. She had lost that grey dullness in her eyes and there was a hint of a spring in her step once again. She had started to rethink her life. Did she still want to be a solicitor and return to all the demands that the job entailed? She had tasted the freedom of a different life here with Barney. But she couldn't survive without some sort of order in her life surely?

After a few more weeks, Barney told Claire that he would be leaving for Dublin the next weekend. He'd been to the Temple Bar area many times before and he knew that his fiddle playing was always in demand in the pubs there whatever the season. Claire took the news as inevitable but that night was unable to sleep, lying awake until the early hours.

'What shall I do, Smithy?' she said to her canine companion at the foot of her bed. 'Will you think I'm mad if I just up-sticks and move on and follow Barney?'

Smithy opened his eyes, yapped once and went back to sleep.

'I'll take that as a 'No, you're not mad' then, shall I?' laughed Claire.

On their morning walk to the beach the next day, Claire and Smithy almost ran to Barney's hut – she'd made up her mind. She would lock up the house and accompany her fiddler friend to Ireland. She'd start to take risks too, just like Barney. She'd spent the night picturing his face when she told him what she'd planned to do. She couldn't wait to tell him.

When they arrived at the hut, it was locked; she was too late. Barney had already packed up and gone. Claire rattled the latch and started banging on the door.

'No, no, Barney! You can't leave me and Smithy behind,' she cried.

Smithy started barking in sympathy with Claire. The night-time anguish over the biggest decision she'd made in her life was all in vain. She knew then that she wouldn't see her travelling musician again. She knew that life on the road was all that Barnabus Hopkins knew and she reasoned with herself that he wouldn't have wanted the responsibility of taking along someone he'd only just met a few weeks ago. Claire felt sad and a little wistful but was surprised that this feeling of sadness was nothing like the huge black cloud of depression that had been enveloping her for months. She patted Smithy and hugged him.

'Do you know, Smithy? Although Barney's left us, I actually think I've moved on with my life. Meeting Barney was good for me. I've learned to take a few risks and not take things too seriously,' she whispered. 'Come on; let's drag ourselves back up that hill.'

Smithy did his usual trick of running round in circles, chasing his tail and barking until they set off for home. Claire smiled. She looked back at the hut which seemed so desolate and empty now and wondered what might have been if she'd gone to Ireland with Barney. She would never know now.

Barney walked along the deck of the ferry and looked back at the diminishing grey-green shapes he was leaving behind. The sun was just appearing and the ship was almost deserted at that time of the morning.

'I wonder if she knows I've gone yet,' he thought, sadly. Never before had he found it so hard to leave a place. Never before had he enjoyed the company of another human being quite so much as he had hers.

'I did it for you, Claire,' he said out loud. 'It wouldn't have been the life for you, my love. It may seem exciting now but you'd soon have come to hate it; not knowing where you'll rest your head, not knowing where the next meal will come from, having no home comforts, moving on every few weeks. You could have ended up hating me even.'

Barney breathed out slowly, brushed away a tear and started to play a haunting melody on his beloved violin. But then he'd be back playing down at The Island again next summer, wouldn't he?

5
THE BUTTON BOX
Tina K Burton

Mollie stopped sorting through her belongings, went into the kitchen to make a cup of tea then took it through to sit at the dining table for a much-needed break. Her old bones weren't what they used to be, it took her twice as long to do anything nowadays. She gave a sigh and looked around at the half packed boxes, paper, bubble wrap and her possessions scattered over every available surface. How she would miss this house!

Her gaze fell on the pretty, but old and faded box at the end of the table. She stared at it for a while before sliding it towards her and removing the lid. It was her old button box. She wondered whether she'd need it anymore. She was hardly likely to do any more dressmaking with her eye sight being so bad, and it would just take up space – space that she wouldn't have in her new flat.

Spotting a blue button, she picked it up and searched out its pink companion as the memories of Paul and Caroline's little cardigans, knitted by Mollie's mother Grace, flooded her mind.

The twins had been born over fifty-five years ago, but it seemed like only yesterday. She could picture those cardigans hanging side by side on the washing line with all the other baby clothes, blowing gaily in the wind.

She took a sip of tea, then selected a small pearl button, which immediately transported her back to her wedding day. She couldn't have wished for a more perfect day. The sun shone its face upon the love-struck couple as they danced out of church for the photos; Mollie, in her beautiful dress with its tiny pearl buttons down the back, and Jack looking very smart in his new suit. She could still picture his face as he looked down at her - the love in his eyes. She remembered how happy she'd been that day; looking forward to the promise of a future together with the man she adored.

Smiling at the memory, she searched through the aged box for another button.

This one was a cream fabric covered button, and held no specific memories as such, except that it was very old, and from one of her mother's wedding shoes.

Grace was no longer around, but holding the button in her hand, Mollie could conjure up her image. The soft, wispy white hair, kind blue eyes and the way she always smelt of violets. She'd loved violet perfume, and Mollie had bought her some every Christmas. Now, whenever she came across the familiar scent, it made her feel all warm and comfortable as she remembered her gentle mother.

Mollie pushed her fingers around the box, enjoying the feel of the different textured buttons; some shiny and smooth, some course and hard, some with scalloped edges, some soft with fabric, until she found one which wasn't as old as the last. Round, with a green centre and gold edge, it was from a suit that she wore when Caroline got married. She still had the hat somewhere too. It was a lovely, if eventful day. The car broke down on the way to the church, meaning that the bride was more than fashionably late. Her husband-to-be, Tom, paced up and down, beside himself with worry, thinking that she'd decided to jilt him at the altar. The guests all burst into laughter at the relief on his face when Caroline flew into the church flushed and flustered. Thankfully, the rest of the day went without a hitch.

All thoughts of packing now forgotten, Mollie then took out another button. Small, flower shaped, and made from Mother of Pearl, it came from Mollie's first grandchild's christening gown. What a day that was!

A boiling hot afternoon in July, the church interior wasn't cool as they usually are, but unbearably stuffy, with no air. The baby cried non-stop, desperate to be freed from the confines of her gown, and the Vicar had to halt the proceedings whilst someone fetched him a glass of water because he almost fainted. Heat-stroke was the diagnosis. He wasn't too amused when Tom suggested having a drink from the font to speed things up! The look on his face was priceless, and Mollie had to stifle a laugh. It certainly wasn't the thing to do - laughing in church, especially in front of the vicar.

Poor Caroline, nothing ever seemed to be straightforward for her, but luckily, she saw the funny side later.

Mollie frowned as she picked up another button, trying to place it. She thought for a moment, then smiled. Of course, how could she have forgotten? It was one of the most satisfying days of her life – Paul's passing out parade with the RAF. She felt that she must have been the proudest mother there that day watching her son; and she shed some tears too. She just couldn't help it; he looked so handsome in his uniform. Even Jack'd had a lump in his throat.

That had been a decision and a half for her, deciding what to wear. She'd wanted to look her best, didn't want to let Paul down, but had put on weight; middle aged spread Jack teasingly said, so none of her suits fitted. After many hours shopping, with a grumpy Jack telling her that everything she'd tried on looked nice, she finally settled on a duck egg blue suit, with four big square buttons on the jacket. She had to find a hat to match too of course, But Jack escaped that shopping trip, and Mollie took Caroline instead. It turned into a lovely day, with afternoon tea at a rather posh restaurant later.

Mollie replaced it and searching through the box, took out one final button. Rather plain, round, brown and not even shiny anymore, it was probably the best and worst button in the whole box. The old lady held it for a few moments, squeezing her eyes shut as tears welled up, then she opened them and tried to focus on it as the tears spilled over and slid down her wrinkled cheeks. This button was a spare one from the suit Jack wore when they got married all those years ago, the same suit he'd been buried in six months ago.

She put the lid back on the box with a sigh, her hand absentmindedly caressing the top of it. Her mother had started collecting buttons soon after she got married, snipping them off old garments or shoes, ready to be used on something else; except, she never did use them. She just kept them in this hexagon shaped box, which Mollie could remember playing with as a small child.

Mollie made her decision. Her impending move to a smaller place meant she just couldn't take everything with her. She had to be ruthless and either throw things away or give them to the charity shop. Maybe it was time to let go of the past and move on.

However, as she looked at it, she knew she couldn't completely get rid of the box with its buttons of different shapes, sizes and colours; some very ordinary, some unusual and pretty. She realised that this wasn't just a box of buttons. It was a box of treasured memories.

More than a lifetime of nostalgia and precious moments lay in those buttons, and Mollie knew just what to do with it. The time had come to pass it down to her daughter, just as Grace had done with her. That way, she'd still be able to see it and share her memories. And if Caroline added to it over time, she could pass it down to her daughter too; eventually there could be generations of memories, all held in the buttons of a worn and faded old box.

6
THE END-OF-THE-PIER SHOW
Derek Haycock

The sun's rays burst through ribbed clouds; sheets of light splayed out across the wrinkled foil of the North Sea. On the raised promenade, an old man stopped and put his hand to his forehead as if in salute. 'You don't see that in Hounslow,' he said, apparently unaware his female companion had walked on.

After a few steps, without him to shield her from the easterly wind, the short woman turned round. The hem of her brown coat and the back of her shiny headscarf flapped as she called out. 'Come on. I'm freezing. What are you doing now?'

The wind chopped at his words. 'The light, Maureen, you don't... see that... at home.'

'You probably would if you took your nose out the newspaper once in a while.'

Back by her side, he tried to take her gloved hand, but she shook him off with a rebuke. 'What are you up to? Get out of it. What'll people think?'

'That we're happily married, which is what we are, isn't it?'

'You needn't think you can get round me that easily, Jack Fenton. Coming to Suffolk for two days is no compensation for not going to Florida.'

'It's the credit crunch. I told you about the exchange rate. Soon it'll be a dollar to the pound. Best to wait, love.'

He bit at his bottom lip; the grey whiskers of his slender moustache bunched against the skin.

They walked slowly. On their left, the variously coloured beach huts provided distraction for Jack. 'You'd think these would be made more use of on a Saturday. They cost a good penny, I bet.'

'It's always money with you. After all we've been through in the last year – losing both girls in that way.'

'I-I know, love. It's hard for me, too.'

'It's always worse for a woman. They were my girls. My little girls.' She stopped, and opened her handbag. After finding a tissue, she tilted her glasses up and dabbed at her eyes.

'We'll go next year, Maureen – credit crunch or no credit crunch.' He took the tissue from her and put it in his coat pocket. 'I promise.'

'I'll believe it when I see it,' she said as they continued walking. 'You could at least have brought me to Blackpool. You know I like Blackpool.'

'You said you hated Blackpool.'

'That was then... Sometimes, I think you just don't know anything about me. Fifty-six years of marriage and you still know nothing.'

He shook his head. 'Okay, Blackpool it is, next year.'

'See! I knew it. Florida is gone already. Typical – bloody Blackpool.'

'Wherever you want. A bond matures in December. I'll have a little extra to spend.'

'You and your money.'

'I do, you know, love'

'You do what?'

'Know you, I mean. I do know you.'

'You don't show it.'

Jack put his arm round her. 'That's not fair, love.'

'You're at it again. You can't get round me like that. If you think there's going to be any funny business tonight... That shop's long shut. You can put those thoughts out of your mind right away.'

'Ah... As if I don't know...'

'You men are all the same. A bit of sea air and you get frisky.'

He moved his arm to take hold of hers and turn her towards him. 'That's not fair, Maureen. Do I ever comp –' Looking into her eyes, something made him stop. 'You're teasing me.'

'You daft old bugger,' she said, with the hint of a smile.

He looked towards the sea. 'Let's go swimming. Those boys are going in. We can buy some costumes and towels up by the pier.'

The more Maureen took in the scene – the steps down to the pebble-strewn beach; the youths goose-stepping into waves having left their clothes drooped over a wooden groyne, which stapled the land to the sea – the more she shrank into her coat.

'You got me in there once. You won't catch me again.'

'I had to propose to you that time, didn't I?' Jack rubbed his palms together and grinned. 'We'll be fine. It would be better if we had one of these huts, though. We'll just have to manage without. A bit of shingle between the toes. Nothing like it.'

'You're not serious, Jack. It's only April. That water'll be far too cold.'

He chuckled. 'I'm pulling your leg. You deserved it.'

Maureen's lips pursed. 'I'm not in the mood. Are we going to walk to the pier or not?'

'The stroll will do us good. I promise I won't get

frisky.'

'I suppose I should count myself lucky you didn't try to get me up that bloomin' lighthouse.'

Jack turned and stared at the tall, white cone, which dominated the nearby townscape. 'I wouldn't do that. Not on our first day. We'll do that in the morning before we head off.'

Maureen's pout quivered. 'I'm not in the mood for your monkey business. You just don't know me. My feet are hurting.' She turned from him and resumed walking northwards.

'I'm sorry, love. I didn't mean...' he said, catching up with her.

She had stopped to stare at a hearse, which moved slowly along the adjacent coastal road that was lined on the far side by terraced 'bed and breakfast' houses.

The long windows of the hearse were packed with flowers, and the rear window was filled with a display spelling out MUM in white carnations. The pale, wooden coffin was barely revealed.

'It's gaudy, that is,' Maureen said. 'Now that is a waste. They should have given the money to charity.' She tightened her grip on the handle of her handbag, the imitation leather of her glove glistening as it stretched over swollen knuckles.

Jack looked about him before putting his mouth close to Maureen's ear. 'Shhhhh, love. Someone might hear. Each to their own.'

* * *

'I suppose you'll be wanting fish and chips,' Maureen said, staring into the custard-coloured café that formed part of the pier's frontage. 'That's what this is about. Always thinking of your stomach.'

'I'm not bothered. See how we feel later.'

Maureen's face took on a wistful look. 'Well, what about me? I'm hungry now.'

'Let's walk to the end and back first. It won't take long. And I think there's a nicer restaurant on the pier, with tables outside.'

Maureen didn't move as her husband approached the start of the boardwalk.

'We don't have to sit outside,' he said.

'You needn't shout.'

Jack's heavy eyebrows slid together. He put his hands into his coat pockets and stared at the ground. Maureen's voice made him look up.

She was in front of him. 'Why do you want to walk all the way to the end? Are you going to jump off?'

'You'd probably like that – me disappearing under the waves.'

'At least it would be interesting!'

'What do you mean?'

'You've no imagination, Jack. Never have had. Over forty years selling papers and now you spend your last years bloomin' reading them.'

Jack's eyes widened. 'No imagination, is it?' he said. 'Look out there, near the horizon.' His arm pointed out to sea.

'I can't see anything.'

'That tanker or whatever it is. The big boat with the pink band along the bottom of its hull. They are regular along this stretch.'

'What about it?'

'It's from Holland, that is. Full of Dutch pirates who've come to steal the pink marshmallows from the café near the end of the pier.'

43

'What?'

'That's why it's pink. Those buggers have taken all the marshmallows.'

'You're bonkers... Marshmallows.'

'Sophie liked that story, when we came here a couple of years ago.'

'Did she, Jack? I wish Tracy, Tony and Sophie were here now. Best neighbours we've ever had. It would have been nice to have a youngster around.'

'They were all youngsters compared to us.'

'I wonder how they're getting on up north.'

'Have to go where the work is nowadays.' Jack shrugged, and gave a reflective smile. 'Ay... I miss little Sophie.'

'What about our girls? They loved this, too. You never talk about them.'

'Don't I?'

'You've got me all upset now. You don't know me at all.'

'I didn't mean...'

'That's your problem. You never do. You never do.'

'We'll have a cup of tea, later. That'll buck us up.'

He took her arm and coaxed her onto the pier. 'The sooner we get to the end, the sooner we can come back and have that tea.'

The shingle below them, dark with shadow between the grey decking boards, gave way to wallowing, brown-green water as the couple passed the pier's restaurant. Chatting diners, seated out at plastic tables, seemed not to notice their progress. Aromas of coffee and vinegar carried on the salty breeze. A gull circled, squawking, overhead.

'It's too windy for this,' Maureen said. 'I'm going to

lose my scarf if it gets any worse.'

'We can watch the water clock, if you like. It's coming up to the hour.'

'What's that then?'

'Half-way along... Past the shop.'

'I don't know, Jack. What's the point?'

'Just a bit of fun.'

* * *

A crowd was gathered in front of the water clock, which was a nonsense-assembly of levers, spouts and twisted-iron figurines. Some of the people spoke in Dutch.

As the hour struck, linked parts went into their clanking routine, swivelling and spraying water, this time onto blond children who went too close. It was towards these excited, dancing and jumping figures that Maureen and Jack stared in silence.

'Okay,' Jack said, once the crowd had dispersed. 'Show over.'

'I want to go back to the B and B. I've had enough for one day.'

'The end is only a few yards farther. It would be a shame not to make it.'

Jack put his arm round Maureen's shoulders. She didn't complain, perhaps not even noticing. As before, they walked slowly, but now in step with each other, and with their shoulders slumped like those of soldiers at the end of a long march. Trailing them, their compressed shadow rippled as it slid over the grooved decking.

They approached the last of the shed-like structures that beaded the pier. This one, doors wide open, was evidently reserved for a coming wedding party. Floral displays and white-clothed tables announced a new beginning for another couple.

'Look,' Maureen said, peering in through the door.

'They couldn't have done that in our day. The old pier was close to falling down.'

'You proposed to me under it!'

'It was the only place I could get you to myself.' Jack's arm tightened around Maureen.

'Half the print works came on the coach. We had friends then.'

'And don't forget your fussing Aunt Muriel,' Jack said.

'She was good to us when we got married. If it wasn't for her, we wouldn't have had our reception.'

'Victoria sponge and a glass of sherry in her parlour.'

'It's more than your family did for us.'

'We'd better move on before we're seen being nosey.'

'Typical – because I'm interested in something that you're not.' Maureen stepped further into the doorway, causing Jack to release her.

'It's not that.'

'What then?'

'I'm keen to...'

'What?'

Jack looked towards the pier's end. 'Just something...' His words dissolved in the wind.

The pier ended in a broad cross-piece that served as a boarding jetty; there was a gate in the end rail. A nearby notice advertised, months in advance, departure of a daytrip cruise to London.

From the northern side of the cross-piece, two men were angling with long rods. Boxes of bait and fishing tackle were open by their feet.

Jack led Maureen to the end. His bony hand skimmed along the rail, fingers twitching like a pianist's, until settling next to the fixture for a life belt. He put his other arm round her. 'We made it,' he said, gazing towards the sea. 'I'm sorry it's cold.'

Maureen said in a weak voice, 'It would have been nice to have had children, wouldn't it?' She said it almost absently, in a way that conveyed the weariness of repetition.

Jack drew her closer. 'Look at this.' He moved his hand from the rail. In so doing he revealed an oblong plate, just one in a stream of brass plaques that lined the railing.

After reading the engraving, Maureen asked, 'When did you do that?'

'Soon after the girls died.'

'How?'

'I phoned up, then sent a cheque. I was lucky there was a space.'

Jack polished the brass with his handkerchief. 'I told you I know you.'

'It's perfect, Jack. "In loving memory of Pixie and Trixie, our precious Scotties. Run free, girls, Mum and Dad".'

Maureen put her arm round Jack's back.

After a few minutes, he said, 'It's as if we're standing on the bow of a ship, like the couple in that film you liked.'

She looked up at him. 'Where are you taking us, Captain?'

'Where do you want to go?'

She thought for a few seconds, and then sighed. 'Somewhere with volcanoes, Jack – and waves with real white horses.'

'I know of just the place. You can wear a grass skirt and have flowers in your hair.'

* * *

Maureen took his hand. 'Not too many flowers, Jack. I don't like too many flowers.'

'I know, love.' He kissed her forehead. 'Shall we have some hot chocolate now?'

'Yes, love, that would make a nice change.'

'Perhaps there'll be marshmallows, too.'

7
MARIE'S NECKLACE
Annette Siketa

The audacious weekend theft made headlines around the world - 'Priceless Marie Antoinette Necklace Stolen'. On Monday morning, the newspaper office was still buzzing when Teresa Piccolo arrived at work. Ordinarily cheerful and fresh faced, her uncharacteristic gaunt and dishevelled appearance, might have been mistaken for the flu.

A veteran newspaper man, Editor Harold Bartlet, was still doggedly pursuing the story, when he saw Teresa approaching his office. Her lifeless eyes and trance-like state, were enough to tell him that something was terribly wrong. He opened the door and beckoned her inside.

"My goodness, Teresa, you look awful. Please, sit down."

Teresa did not accept the invitation. Instead, with a jerky, almost painful movement, she withdrew a glittering object from her pocket and placed it on his desk. Sprawled across the blotter, their brilliance mocking the florescent lighting, were over 100 diamonds, and over 200 years of history.

Harold stared in disbelief. He was almost afraid to touch it. "Where on earth did you get this?" he asked in a shocked whisper, tentatively picking up the necklace. The overall design was reminiscent of a flattened chandelier, with five rows of incremental stones. It was surprisingly heavy, and to the untrained eye, the perfectly cut faceted diamonds, could have been mistaken for cut glass.

Silent tears slid down Teresa's pale pinched face. "I didn't steal it, I found it."

Harold covered the necklace with the morning paper, its headline ironically proclaiming the theft, and guided Teresa to a seat. "Wait here," he ordered, and left the office. He returned with two mugs of coffee, turned a sign on the door to read 'closed' – a private 'in' joke, then extracted a digital dictaphone from a drawer. "Teresa, I want you to tell me everything that happened at the museum. Omit nothing."

Teresa sipped the reviving coffee, which Harold had made sweet and strong. She wrapped her hands tightly around the mug, but kept her eyes downcast. "I knew Saturday was my last chance to see the exhibition before it returned to France. The queue was so long that it wound around the block. When I finally entered the Marie Antoinette display room, there were signs everywhere saying 'No images of any description', and 'No standing'. Security kept everyone moving, which meant you only saw each piece for a few seconds. I then went to the gift shop, which was overflowing with paraphernalia on the French revolution. The shop was packed, but I managed to select a book, a DVD, and several other trinkets."

"The exhibition was more popular than the museum anticipated," said Harold. "They must have made a fortune from merchandising alone. But please, go on."

"The assistant had just handed me the bag containing my purchases when, just to the left of me, a man and woman began arguing in a foreign language. Somehow, the woman lost her balance, and the next thing I knew, we were both on the floor. An elderly man helped me stand up. He picked up my bag and asked if I was alright. My elbow was a bit sore, but otherwise I was fine."

Harold held up a hand. "Have you ever seen any of these people before? Think carefully."

The ghost of a smile touched Teresa's lips. For the past 36 hours, she had done nothing *but* think. "No, never."

"Go on."

"I left the museum and drove to the market. I wandered round for a while and then went home. Later that evening, I decided to watch the DVD I'd bought. I distinctly remember that I was sitting on the floor when I tipped up the bag. And there it was, the necklace, sprawled across my carpet like some grotesquely glittering spider."

Harold slowly nodded in approval. It was an apt description. "What happened next?"

For the first time since entering the office, Teresa's face showed signs of colour. "In order to understand that, I have to tell you a little story. I have always admired strong willed women from history, such as Catherine the Great, Cleopatra, and indeed, Marie Antoinette herself. However, the closest I've ever been to any of them, was when I went to London last year and visited the tomb of Elizabeth I in Westminster Abbey."

Harold smiled. "I remember that. You didn't shut up about it for weeks."

"Yes," said Teresa, "but there's something I didn't tell you. Because of an elaborate security railing, it's very difficult to see the Queen's marble coffin, let alone her effigy on top. I managed to get my fingers through the bars and..." she momentarily faltered, "well I know this is going to sound crazy, but I received a sort of electric shock, as though the Queen herself was telling me not to touch. The thing is, when I touched the necklace, I had the same peculiar sensation. Yes I know I should have rung the police there and then, and with the benefit of hindsight, I wish to god I had, but foolishness and vanity got the better of me, and after convincing myself that nobody would miss it for one night, I…um…put it on."

Teresa paused to drink more coffee. Raising the mug to her lips, she half expected to see her boss looking at her reproachfully, but instead, Harold Bartlet was fingering the necklace. She wondered if he was trying to experience the same sensation.

"We can deal with the police shortly," said Harold. "Right now, I'm more interested in you. There's obviously more to this story, so please continue."

"I don't know how to describe what happened next. I have never experienced anything like it. The closest analogy I can ascribe, is that it was like having a digital camera inside my head. I was perfectly aware of who I was and my surroundings, yet roughly every ten minutes or so, a different picture popped into my head.

Harold had a fair idea of what Teresa was trying to describe, and although he was reluctant to break her concentration, it was important legally, historically, and commercially, to assimilate the facts. "Do you mean like an old fashioned slide show?"

"Yes, that's it," she said with a spark of enthusiasm. "Do you remember those famous pictures of Kate Winslet wearing a red dress in the movie titanic? Well my pictures were like that, only in this case, everyone was wearing 18th century costume."

Harold left the office for a few minutes to refill the mugs. He also wanted to give Teresa time to compose herself. His hound dog instinct told him that whatever was to come, it was painful. "I don't think too many men would object if the delightful Miss Winslet popped into their heads every few minutes, but I understand your point. How long did these flashes occur?"

Teresa took the offered mug. "I haven't finished yet," she said quietly. "The flashes as you called them, were giving me a headache, so I played the DVD I bought, 'A History of Versailles', and things became even stranger. As I watched, I was overwhelmed by a feeling of, ironically as the French call it, déjà-vous. As the camera panned around the rooms, I could have sworn I'd seen them before. The paintings, the statues, the gardens, they all seemed so extraordinarily familiar, and yet I've never set foot in the place."

Harold chewed the end of a pencil. In his opinion, Teresa was a perfectly rational and intelligent woman, which is what made her story all the more interesting, perhaps even frightening. He had no doubt she believed every word. "Had you ever been to Versailles, I'd have said you were suffering from a severe bout of nostalgia. What did you do next?"

"The DVD finished and I went to bed."

"Were you still wearing the necklace?"

Teresa's face reddened slightly. "Yes." She swallowed hard. "And in every respect, that's when the real nightmare began. I can't say for certain whether I was actually asleep, but in any event, the flashes became faster and faster until eventually, they all joined together to form a sort of movie, complete with sounds and smells. The next thing I knew, I couldn't breathe. My hair had become tangled in the necklace and it was choking me – see?" She gingerly pulled back the collar of her shirt. A raised red line the thickness of a shoelace, completely encircled her neck.

Harold frowned as he examined the wound. He was about to suggest it had been made by a garrotte, but thought this imprudent. "And you say the necklace did this? How odd." He took numerous shots with a digital camera and then resumed his seat.

Teresa stared sightlessly into her coffee. "I've barely slept since. Every time I close my eyes, it's there, in grand technicolour detail." Disposing of the mug, she put her head in her hands and began to cry. "I must be mad. I don't know what to do."

Harold stood up and patted her shoulder. "Well the first thing we have to do, is lock this baby away." He deposited the necklace in a safe. "Teresa, I want you to recall the last full dream. I know it's upsetting, but try to describe everything you saw, no matter how insignificant."

Teresa shuddered and drew in a deep steadying breath. "I am in a room at Versailles. There is a large painting of Diana the Huntress on the wall. I'm wearing a pink satin dress with silver and blue bows, and there is an elaborate but heavy wig on my head. I am frightened because I can hear an angry mob outside the window. I hurry to a honey coloured cabinet which has many narrow drawers, and put my hands on a rear carved panel. I press down hard and the top springs open, revealing a secret cavity. It is crammed with documents and jewels."

"Just a minute," said Harold quickly. "Do you know what the documents are?"

Teresa shook her head. "No. I did remove something from the cavity, although I couldn't tell you what it was, but it definitely wasn't a document."

"Is it possible that the cabinet was on the DVD, and that somehow, it became part of the other thing?"

Teresa tried to think, but sleep deprivation and apprehension, were hampering concentration. "I don't think so."

Harold slowly nodded his head. The germ of an idea was formulating in his mind, but he did not want to give it voice, at least, not yet. "Go on," he urged.

Her eyes brimming with tears, Teresa looked pleadingly at her boss. "I really don't want to, it was horrible."

"Take it from an old newspaper man, you'll feel much better once you get it off your chest."

Teresa summoned her courage. He was right of course, but it didn't make it any easier. "I am in the Bastille, and a young woman is helping me to bathe. A guard is watching our every move, and when I plead for pity and decency, he sneers and spits on the floor. Another man enters carrying a pair of scissors, and without regard to my personage, hacks off my long white wispy hair. The scene shifts to the early hours before my execution. I am wearing a plain white dress, black stockings, and plum coloured shoes. The insidious republican government are so terrified that, even in my final hours, I might prove an instrument for subversiveness, that they have denied me paper and ink. Now I'm standing in a doorway with my hands bound behind my back. I can see thousands of people and am very frightened, not because I'm about to die, but because given the chance, they'd tear me apart. An old rickety cart appears. I am ordered to get in and sit with my back to the horses, which is a great insult, and as it moves off, much to the delight of the jailers and onlookers, I almost topple over."

Outside his glass panelled door, Harold saw that his sub-editor, Josh Turnbull, was trying to attract his attention. Harold waved him away with a vehement flick of his wrist. Teresa's eyes had become sightless again. Moreover, she was breathing hard and her hands had balled into white knuckled fists. Wherever her mind was, it was not in a busy newspaper office in the middle of a thriving city. Indeed, as she continued her narrative, Harold wondered if it was Teresa herself speaking, for her voice was strong and defiant.

"My final journey is humiliating. The crowd is so thick that I can barely see the ground. Most are dirty and dishevelled and dressed in rags. The smell is overpowering, a nauseating mix of raw sewage and sweat. Women spit and hurl obscenities at me, but what the people do not realise, is that I welcome my death, for it will end my suffering and misfortune. To the surprise of many, I bound up the steps to the scaffold. Several officials, their expressions cruel and grim, are waiting to witness my death. A priest is attempting succour by reading from the revised bible, but as I do not approve of the republic's new doctrine, I ask him to leave. I prefer to meet my god with my soul and conscience unsullied. I have heard it said that when the blade slices through the neck, anyone standing too close will be sprayed with blood. In addition, as it drips through the cracks in the scaffold, dogs will greedily lick it up. I try not to think of this as I take my final steps, nor of the thousands of people who are waiting for me to falter. But I will not give them satisfaction! I remain steadfast and courageous and do not ask for instruction. I look at the sky for the last time, and pray that a sympathetic god awaits. I willingly place my head on the guillotine and close my eyes. My last thoughts are of my mother, my husband, my children, and what might have been." Teresa swayed slightly as she came back to consciousness. "That's it, that's all there is."

Summoning his own faculties, Harold turned the dictaphone off. "The police will want a full statement of course. However, before we do anything formal, I'm going to contact the French embassy. I think they would be very interested in your story. Go home Teresa, I'll contact you later."

Teresa did not need to be told twice, yet despite being exhausted to the point of collapse, upon arriving home, there was something she urgently wanted to check. She ran the DVD in double-quick time. She had been right, there was no cabinet matching her description on the disc. In addition, the feeling of familiarity she had experienced when first watching it, had gone.

Back in the office, Josh Turnbull stared open mouthed at the glittering object in Harold's hand. "And that's not all," he said, returning the necklace to the safe, "listen to this." Harold played the recording in its entirety, neither man speaking until it had finished. "If anyone else had come to me with that story," said Harold, smiling in bemusement at his stunned sub-editors face, "I would have sent them for a drug test."

"It's incredible. It's almost as though Teresa was actually there. An eyewitness account if you will. It would make a terrific story."

Harold raised an inquiring eyebrow. "Under what category? Features, world events, or psychic corner?"

Josh looked suitably rebuked. "So, what do we do about it?"

"For the moment – nothing. However, I have placed a call to the French embassy."

"And the police? Surely they'll have to be told."

Harold grinned and said cryptically, "Not just yet. I'm calling in a favour. I do want somebody from the police to hear the recording, but I don't want them to act until I've spoken to the embassy."

Josh looked concerned. "Why? We could get into serious trouble for withholding evidence."

Harold leaned back and folded his hands, a supercilious smile on his face. "Let's just call it, gut instinct."

Josh stood up to leave. "You know boss, the shift in context is fascinating, as though instead of being an eyewitness, Teresa actually became the Queen."

Harold slowly nodded his head. "I agree, and that's what makes it so powerful." The phone rang. "Not a word to anyone, Josh," he added, and picked up the receiver.

Teresa was dreaming again. She was in a large greenhouse surrounded by rows of seedlings. Beside her, was a tall well-built man wearing a white shirt with an elaborate lace cravat, a blue satin coat with silver piping, and black shoes with diamond-studded buckles. His long black hair was a mass of curls, and his charming smile was enhanced by a perfectly trimmed moustache. He muttered words she could not understand, then taking her into his arms, began to kiss her passionately.

At 9.30 the next morning, Teresa, Josh Turnbull, Tim Murray – the newspapers legal advisor, and Detective Sergeant John Agostino, were all seated in Harold's office. The recording had just finished. Tim Murray said, "There are a number of questions to be answered, not the least being, who put the necklace in the bag."

Harold said, "The museum would have run the security tapes by now," and looked at John Agostino for confirmation. The dark and swarthy Detective nodded his head.

"That's the first thing they would have done."

"There are two distinct aspects to the recording," Tim went on, "the first being the theft itself. I think we can safely leave that in the hands of the police. The second, is Teresa's extraordinary description."

Teresa felt a rush of annoyance, for the latter had been said with a note of scepticism. She scowled and crossed her arms. "I am not crazy, I am not on drugs, and no it's not that time of the month."

Tim smiled indulgently. "I am very pleased to hear it, but I was about to ask what we should do about it. Can we confirm your description from historical records?"

Josh said, "I'll surf the Internet and do some research."

Tim addressed John Agostino. "As Teresa and Harold have both handled the necklace, would their fingerprints and DNA erase any other that might be there?"

"Not necessarily. Every surface will be examined in minute detail."

Teresa said, "Will I be arrested?"

John turned to face her. "If the museum security tapes confirm your story, then I should say not. May I look at your neck?" Teresa removed the scarf she'd been wearing, and being at such close quarters, she was absolutely sure they had never met before, yet his face was vaguely familiar. "You will still need to make a statement," said John as he examined the wound, "But if I were you..." he gave her an ingratiating smile, "...and if you repeat this I'll deny it, I'd stick to the salient facts."

Harold said, "Before any official questioning begins, Teresa and I have an appointment with the secretary to the French ambassador. In fact, we should be leaving very soon."

Teresa stood up. "If you will excuse me, I'll just visit the ladies before we go," and left the office.

The moment the door was closed, John looked directly at Harold. "I can't explain it, but that wound looks remarkably like a burn, and although there's no blistering, I'd really like a doctor to see it."

"Teresa says it doesn't hurt, but I'll make sure she sees one when we return. One more thing, and I know it's stretching the friendship, but could you look at those security tapes yourself? It is the only thing that will categorically prove her innocence."

Tim frowned as he said, "Do you doubt her story?"

"If you mean do I think she's guilty, then no, I have no doubts. You did not see her yesterday. The woman who sat in this office, was not Teresa Piccolo."

Teresa and Harold took a taxi to the embassy. "Two things, Teresa," said Harold as they were ushered through security, "firstly, where possible, let me do the talking."

"Gladly."

"Secondly, if you're asked any questions, stick strictly to the facts. Do not mention this morning's meeting."

Harold and Teresa were shown into the comfortably appointed office of the secretary to the French ambassador. Harold said respectfully, "Thank you for seeing us at such short notice."

The impeccably dressed Frenchman, came out from behind his desk and shook their hands. "Guy Rochford," he said amiably, "but please, call me Guy." He gestured to two leather armchairs. "Any information leading to the recovery of the necklace, is of great importance to my government. As you might be aware, it is a recently re-discovered national treasure."

Harold said, "I understand it was discovered by accident a couple of years ago."

The diplomat smiled. "In this case, the word accident is subjective. As you know, the Nazis plundered Europe as though it was their own personal shopping mall, and even though much artwork has been recovered, considerably more has not. Yet the Nazis were not the only ones to profit. There are documented cases of Jews, Swedes, and many other nationalities, hiding fortunes in Swiss bank accounts. About three years ago, a major Swiss bank decided to open security boxes that had not been accessed for fifty years or more. Where the owners are now, who can say? Many had been registered under false names. As each box was opened, the contents were examined by a team of experts. I am to understand that several artworks thought missing or destroyed, were also recovered."

"And the necklace was in a box?" prompted Harold.

"Unfortunately, I cannot give specifics," said Guy. "Suffice to say that my government was delighted to have it back."

"Excuse me, Guy," said Teresa. "You just said the government was delighted to have it back, but wasn't it the private property of Marie Antoinette? After her death, why didn't it pass to her surviving heir's or family?"

"A sensible question," he said with a charming smile. "Tell me, do you know what happened to her children?"

"Not really."

"Then allow me to give you a brief history lesson. After the execution, Marie's remains were taken to the same cemetery where her husband, King Louis XVI, had been interred some nine months earlier. As it was midday, she was beheaded at 11 o'clock, the grave diggers went off to eat their lunch, leaving the body and severed head on the grass. While they were away, and at great personal risk, a woman by the name of Marie Grossholtz, took a wax impression of the dead Queen's face. Regrettably, the impression was lost in a fire, but the woman survived, and in later years, became better known as Madame Tussaud."

"Good gracious," said Teresa in surprise. "I didn't know that."

Guy laughed lightly. "Not many people do. Only two of Marie Antoinette's children survived after her death. The first, a son and rightful heir, was Louis Charles. Fortunately, and I'm not being cruel, he only lived for another 18 months. He died in 1795 aged 10, probably from Tuberculosis. The second child, Marie Theresa, lived for many years. However, like her mother, she was used as a political pawn. In 1795 at the age of 17, she was still a prisoner in Paris. France and Austria were at war, and she was basically left to rot. But then the republican government exchanged her for political prisoners, and she was sent to Austria, her mother's homeland. With the benefit of hindsight, she might have done better to stay where she was."

"Why?" asked Teresa, who was thoroughly absorbed.

"Although women were not allowed to succeed to the throne in France, and for all intents and purposes, Austria too, she was still the daughter of a King, and therefore, a valuable marriage pawn. The ruling families of Austria, the Hapsburgs and the Bourbons, began squabbling over which of her first cousins she should marry. Her prospective husband, and she had no say in the matter, had to be of good stock. They eventually chose the Duke d'Aungulem, which proved a disastrous choice. He was cruel and vile, and according to contemporary reports, devoutly homosexual. This probably explains why the marriage was never consummated."

"The poor woman," said Teresa quietly, her eyes sparkling with unshed tears.

Guy paused for a moment then went on, "There is a little known historical footnote here that might interest you. In 1830, her father-in-law, Charles 10th, who had been installed as King of France after the fall of the republic, was forced to abdicate, along with his son. They had to sign a document called 'The Instrument of Abdication', and since then, historians have debated the legality of what happened next. The deposed King signed the document first. The paper was then blotted and his signature checked. But, in the intervening minutes before his son signed, technically, he was King of France."

Teresa stared at the diplomat in wide-eyed amazement. "You mean Marie Antoinette's daughter became Queen of France, albeit for a few minutes?"

Guy shrugged his shoulders with typical French flair. "In my opinion she was, although constitutional experts may argue differently. She died in October 1851 at the age of 73, some sixty odd years after her mother. As she had no children, the direct line from Louis XVI and Marie Antoinette, ended. When you couple this with the forced abdications, it signalled the end of the French monarchy. After that, all royal property, including that later appropriated by Napoleon, became the concern of the government. I hope this rather long winded explanation, answers your original question."

Teresa smiled appreciatively. "Absolutely."

Guy looked at Harold. "You have important information about the necklace?"

Harold put a small CD player on the desk. When the recording had finished, this time, it was Guy Rochford who stared in wide-eyed amazement. "But this is you." Teresa gave a single nod of her head. "May I keep a copy?" he asked.

Harold had no qualms about giving him the disk. The original recording was locked in his safe. "When Teresa and I return to the office, she will make an official report to the police. I will give them the necklace then."

International relations having duly been satisfied, Harold and Teresa returned to the office. They were greeted by an animated Josh Turnbull. "You will never believe what I've discovered."

Harold grinned as he said, "First things first, we're starving, can you organise some food?"

Comfortably ensconced in Harold's office, Josh continued, "The first thing I learned, was how the necklace was discovered."

Harold held up a hand. "We know all about that. The secretary explained it to us."

"Did he now?" said Josh sceptically. "And did he tell you that according to legend, there's not one but three necklaces. Apart from the colour of the gems – red white and blue, which ironically, the republic introduced for their new French flag, they're identical."

"Blue white and red," corrected Harold.

"Is it?" said Teresa.

"Oh yes, and the French are very touchy about that. Go on, Josh."

Josh rolled his eyes. "Alright then, in flag order. The

blue one is made from sapphires and is called, 'The Tears of France'. Its reputed to be in a private collection in the States. The white one is called, 'The Light of France', and we know where that is." He glanced at the safe. "The last one is made from rubies and is called, 'The Blood of France', and nobody knows where it is."

Teresa started to giggle. "Don't tell me, if you put all three together, then something magical happens."

Josh gave her a look of mock surprise. "How did you guess?"

Harold smiled at their shining faces. Regrettably, it had to end. It was time for officialdom to stamp its authority. "If you're ready, Teresa, I'll call the police."

A few days later, Teresa looked up from her computer to see a smiling John Agostino. "Just thought you'd like to know that you've been officially cleared. The security tapes confirm your story."

"And the thief? Did the tape catch him?"

John shook his head. "I have studied that tape inch by inch, pixel by pixel, but I cannot see anyone put the necklace in your bag. It is possible although highly unlikely, that it happened when you went to the market, but as yet, there is no explanation. However, you might be interested to know that the French government is considering giving you a reward."

"Me?" said Teresa in genuine surprise. "What for?"

"For not disposing of it on the black market and legging it with your ill-gotten gains."

Teresa blushed as she laughed. She liked him, he was a nice man. "Well thanks for coming to tell me. I suppose that puts an end to it."

"Does it? What about the dreams? How do you explain those?"

Teresa sighed heavily. "I can't, but on the plus side, they've stopped."

The newspaper office was alive with activity. Nevertheless, John leaned forward and whispered, "Will you have dinner with me?" He liked her, she was a nice lady. Teresa turned crimson with embarrassment, not because of his unexpected invitation, but because she'd suddenly remembered where she'd seen him before.

On the 14th July the following year, Harold Bartlet, Guy Rochford, John Agostino, and his new pregnant wife, Teresa, were in Paris at the personal invitation of the French government, to witness the official hand-over of the necklaces to the Louvre museum. Three women dressed in period costume, each carried a coloured velvet cushion, with the corresponding necklace laid majestically on top.

After his meeting with Harold and Teresa, Guy Rochford had sent a copy of the recording to an old school friend, who just happened to be an assistant curator at Versailles. The friend had subsequently confirmed that the cabinet did indeed exist, but as it was considered of little value, it had been stored away for years. After following Teresa's instructions, the hitherto elusive 'Blood of France', had been found.

Marie Teresa Agostino, was born three months later on the 16th of October. The timing was auspicious, for it was the date in 1793 when Marie Antoinette had been executed. Harold Bartlet would prove a doting godfather, while Guy Rochford, did not stop smiling for years.

As Teresa lay in the hospital bed, her child barely an arm's length away, she now knew the meaning of her last strange dream. At the time, the seedlings, the man, the passionate embrace, had barely registered. Now however, the symbolism could not have been clearer. Moreover, she had never told anyone about it, and nor would she. She was absolutely convinced that, in return for reuniting the necklaces, Marie Antoinette had given her, Teresa, the happiness she was so cruelly denied.

Turning off the light, Teresa looked out of the window at the black velvety sky. The stars were twinkling like diamonds. "Thank you, your majesty," she whispered. "Rest in peace."

8

NICE

Judith Bruton

Every age can be enchanting,
provided you live within it.
~ *Henri Matisse*

Simon simply waited for his pie, watched and wondered why his meal was taking so long to arrive, and why the hotel restaurant was void of other diners.

Across a sea of black linen tablecloths he caught occasional glimpses of a lone waiter traversing the restaurant. Simon amused himself by noting how the white conical serviettes mimicked yachts sailing in a brisk wind; and the harbour view framed in the tall elegant windows was pure Impressionism, albeit overcast today. The vista of sludgy greys made him feel lonelier and increasingly hungry.

'*Monsieur, votre pâté en croute de boeuf!*' The waiter finally arrived balancing a small tray of food and a glass of white wine.

'*Merci.*' Simon murmured. He remembered how he enjoyed practising his schoolboy French when on the *Côte d'Azur* years ago. Unlike then, he resisted asking for the Rosella tomato sauce; he had learnt his subtle Aussie humour was not appreciated here.

'A sip of sauvignon blanc and a view of the Mediterranean—this is the life!' sighed Simon as he tried to cheer up and prepared to sample his long-awaited meal. Without warning, a tear splashed onto the oversized white plate, missing the miniscule beef pie. Then another and another, until his food was awash and he was weeping aloud; fortunately there was no-one to notice as the waiter was busy behind the bar enjoying a *Gauloise*.

Simon realised the Nice of his memories was no longer so nice. Three thugs had eyed off his baggage the previous evening as he arrived at his hotel, and the shops and dirty streets were almost deserted due to yet another economic downturn in Europe. Simon's once-vibrant dreams of spending his later years painting pictures in Nice with Mary had turned black. He could hardly believe his Mary, Mary quite contrary, was now gone and for the first time in over forty years he was alone.

'Time is a cruel thief,' he sobbed as he wiped his eyes and blew into his handkerchief.

Simon took a bite of soggy pie and perused the brochure from his morning visit to the *Musee Matisse*. Vivid images of his holiday with Mary in Nice during the late-sixties flashed through his mind. As a young couple they had lived for several weeks in a Matissean world of pastel colour and long, narrow hotel bedrooms with petite balconies overlooking the ultramarine sea. They revelled in Matisse's paintings of silvery light and plunging perspectives; and loved the artist's visual interplay of interior and exterior views. *This is where we'll retire one day*, they had fantasised over the *menu turistico*.

Simon absent-mindedly devoured the pie in two or three mouthfuls as he read the pamphlet:

In Nice Matisse noticed the new brilliance of black—the black of coffee in the cup vied for his attention with the black of mirror, notebook, bentwood chair and distant umbrella. When mated with the high bright yellow of lemons fresh from the tree and the Art Nouveau sinuosities of bunched anemones, black did wonders for him…

'*Black did wonders for him*—I never knew that,' reflected Simon.

Simon's years as an art critic reviewing conceptual, post-object art, had left him yearning to paint comfortable, colourful pictures of seductive women, sensuous seascapes and exuberant flowers. But his world turned black, very black, when Mary died from a short, devastating illness last year.

'Black doesn't do it for me,' he sniffed.

'*Café noir, monsieur?*' The waiter deftly delivered his drink.

Simon leant on his elbows and stared into the abyss of his short coffee.

As he lamented his loss, a familiar floral fragrance aroused him from despair. Simon cautiously raised his eyes.

Partly obscured by a blue glass vase of bright yellow begonias on the table opposite, sat a young woman in a hat laden with flowers of satin and silk, twirling a pink and green parasol. Her painted face smouldered with rose tints and rouge, crimson lips and purple eyes. She reminded him of a young, tarty version of his Mary.

Instinctively, Simon fumbled for the box of broken pastels he always carried in his travel bag—just in case. He unrolled one of the starched serviettes and began to sketch. His first marks were hesitant, but soon Fauvist colours spread through his veins as he translated the beauty of the moment into blended pigments of myriad hues.

Simon reached for more napkins and quickly covered them with clashes of shape and colour in a celebration of the joy of seeing afresh—before noticing his muse had disappeared. As he glanced around for the mysterious woman, he heard accordions harmonising on the promenade; festive people streamed into the restaurant and the sun lit the sea pure azure.

A sudden urge for something sweet overtook his senses. Simon beckoned the waiter. '*Un caramel crème* please...*et* two spoons.'

Mary was with him requesting her favourite dessert.

9
COFFEE WITH LUNA
Jeff Williams

I arrive in Huffington's class seconds before the great man himself sails into the room. The cables from his laptop dangle like the tentacles of some maladroit sea creature as he mounts the stage.

Should I lend a hand? Three classes of my helping him to download have laid bare his inability with PowerPoint. Also his pathetic choice of passwords. Access to his electronic grade sheet will net me a certain A.

But I hesitate. Assisting 'The Huff' yet again will brand me as a sycophant. Particularly in Luna's eyes. And hers are the only eyes that matter.

She stands chatting with her buds, 'Huffington's groupies', I call them, as they await the professorial cough that will signal we should take our seats. I squeeze past, but feel a touch, lightly against my shoulder blade. When I turn, I see Luna smiling up at me. Luna of the ethereal skirt and wooly cardigan, buttons undone, smiles at me.

"Yes?" I ask her, overwhelmed by the enormity of what just happened. *Physical contact*.

I appear blasé, but my heart is thumping out the drumbeat of desire. One of the back-row nerds distracts me by rushing to the podium. The usurper will have our professor up and running. The lecture could begin at any moment.

I return to her smile, thinking *you touched me, Luna. The*

ball's in your court.

Her entourage steps back, leaving her stranded, like a castaway on a desert isle, not one foot from where I stand. She clutches awkwardly at the handle of her bag.

"The question you asked last lecture..." she begins.

I nod, encouragingly.

"The question you asked about *detrending*..." Again, she allows her sentence to trail away unfinished.

"Basic time series analysis," I reply, willing her to get to the point. "It's not difficult to grasp."

I throw her a lifeline. "If it's properly explained," I continue.

She seizes it.

"It's what I need for my project," she says, all in one breath. A second's pause, and she adds, "You could explain it to me over coffee."

Coughing erupts from the podium. The 'Huff-signal' heralds the start of class. Luna and I disengage. I take my seat beside the far wall and fire up my laptop. I have precisely fifty-minutes, less the initial minutes of Huff start-up time, to learn the ins and outs of Ms Luna *Whatever-her-last-name-might-be.*

Accessing Huff's faculty account is child's play, thanks to the new puppy. I check his granddaughter's Facebook for the spelling. The memorial page to Scooby-Do-1 makes me wonder what kind of man would require the death of a family pet before initiating a password change. I enter 'Scooby-Do-2' and click on the title of our course: *Applied Statistical Time Series Analysis I*. Et voilà! Halfway down the class list who do I spy but 'Luna *Macintyre*'.

I look to the front of the class where Luna sits with her chin cradled in her hands. She beams towards our professor, drinking in his wisdom, as I scrutinize her reddish hair. Irish or Scottish? Either way, it suggests a closet firebrand.

That sits well with me and I decide to increase her mark on last week's test to an A minus. Bring on the butterfly effect. Having Central Park ravaged by a hurricane will be a small price, balanced against easing an ugly B into a glorious A minus for this woman who caressed my shoulder.

I glance again to where she sits, front row center with her BFFs, and find her staring back at me. *Caught in the act, Luna. Admit it. I'm a hunk and you desire me.* She begins a smile, but abandons it, as if embarrassed. She turns her attention to The Huff and his pontification on multiple regression. I turn my attention to her Facebook page. *Time to spill the beans, Luna.*

I begin with boyfriends, past and present. Perspiration runs through the furrows of my brow as I identify potential suitors. False alarms at first. I consign them to the sibling bin: two brothers. I find an older sister. Then I see him. *Jason.*

I hate the guy, that instant. I hate his retro jacket and his weirdo haystack hair color. Most of all, I hate how Jason of the Golden Fleece has his arm around my Luna. The brazen little vixen is encouraging him, tugging at the hem of her gown—which is strapless, of course—to show off her high heels and those gorgeous calves. *Watch yourself, Luna. Your A minus might yet become a D.*

I forgive her. More or less. I'm not the Spanish Inquisition, and the dance is end of term some time ago. One year ago, to be precise. I record the details of this past transgression, with demerits for dating Golden Boy but a generous 9/10 towards experience gained. I also download her grades from Huff's files—her real grades, without my tinkering. *Don't expect me to cut you too much slack, Luna. This is serious statistical analysis.*

So much for the ball gown. Let the bikini search begin!

Whoa. This I'm not prepared for. My Luna has a photo gallery captioned 'Beside the Pool'. I click the 'in-ground pool' box on my database, thus assigning bonus points to the 'family wealth' category. Her dad will need to be an orthodontist to move this any higher. I'll check him later. At the moment, I'm pool side, inspecting the scantily-clad Macintyre clan, and friends. Luna is the hottest, by far. And... surprise. My Luna has a tattoo.

Call me old-fashioned, but I have a sliding scale of points for permanent tattoos. All negative. Vampires and rock musicians populate the more disreputable end of the gamut, unicorns and kittens the other. A quick zoom reveals that Luna has a rose, plus thorns. I record it as negative five, with a further minus one for placement. *Really, Luna.*

For body-piercings, by which I mean the lack thereof, she acquits herself just fine. Luna has zip. I enter zip, and scan her older sister. That will be Luna, three years hence. I'm not in Huffington's class for nothing. Time series projection, our professor tells us ad nauseam, is the science of the future. I should congratulate him on his double entendre, and he should congratulate me on my stellar programming. Commercial dating software, the likes of *LovingTwoSomes* and *ForeverMore*, are Stone Age by comparison.

I return to the screen to check the *funny-girl.com* website for embarrassing photos. Twitter comes next, and she has an account. Cool.

I scan her tweets, sorting them emotively into buckets I've pre-labeled. Sad, happy, angry, ashamed, witty, argumentative, slutty… Three seconds and I have all of Luna's tweetstats to compare against my own. Umpteen thousand strings, 140-characters apiece, merge and load into my spreadsheet.

So far so good, except there's trouble in Huff City. Our professor's on his final slide and about to finish early, which I can't allow. Not with more skeletons to be unearthed, ghosts of Jasons past, questionable relatives, outrageous Pinterest boards. Luna could be a devil-worshipper, or have some bizarre Brazilian shoe fetish. I need to pry further, deeper. I need more time.

I switch to Huff's website, looking for *StatsWorld XIV*—the Super Bowl of advanced statistics. I check the title of his talk last summer: 'The Vector Autoregressive Moving Average Model in a Changing World,' and I raise my hand, waving to attract attention.

"Professor Huffington, is there any common ground between the Vector Autoregressive Moving Average Model and…" And what? I'm stymied for a second, like I've caught Luna's can't-finish-the-end-of-my-sentences disease. Then, with a stroke of genius, I add, "…and *detrending*?"

The rest of the class glares towards me with annoyance. Except for Luna. Her eyes are aglow with admiration. Awe, even. The back-row nerd will be racked with jealously, and struggling, I've no doubt, to create some superbly insightful question of his own.

My delaying tactics work. Huff removes his glasses. He polishes them against his jacket sleeve—a sure indication we're due for ten more minutes, minimum, of Hufferish technobabble. He launches into the basics of moving averages while I continue my quest through the databases of social media, probing the darkest reaches of the web until I'm poised on the brink, a mouse click from the holy grail that will be my destiny, that will decide whether the red-haired beauty of *Applied Statistical Time Series Analysis I* will become *my* red-haired beauty. I click.

Sadly, the JCS—aka Joint Compatibility Score—shows us poles apart. One and a quarter standard deviations, to be exact. Do I need to question this? The math is undeniable, the conclusion clear; and coffee... What would be the point?

I reach for my phone, anxious to spare Ms Macintyre the humiliation of rejection in the presence of her friends. Texting was created for just such moments. I deftly swing the axe to cut the sapling, letting it fall silently in Luna's little corner of the telecommunication forest: *'No coffee,'* I type. I don't add a smiley face.

10
TAKING TIME
Lilliana Rose

'You've got to slow down and take time to smell the roses.' Mum's voice echoed in my head, even though she had passed away over a year ago. I sat in my car drumming my fingers on the steering wheel to the thoughts. I had turned off the radio so I didn't have to hear once more how hot the day had been. Traffic was bumper to bumper. To try and cool down I had wound down the windows and put the fan on high. But that didn't help much. The air conditioning in my blue Suzuki was dead.

'Smell the roses. How else will you find someone at the 100 miles per hour you always travel?' Mum's voice wasn't helping me to keep calm and cool on the drive home. She never cared I had manage to own a successful business at thirty. I knew she was proud, but Mum always wanted me to find someone after my divorce three years ago. Family was important to me and something I wanted for my future. But for now it was on hold while I tried to put myself back together.

I looked out the window resisting the urge to beep my horn at the car in front. Today had been full of problems to solve and ended with me calling a meeting later tonight. I wanted to be moving not stuck in traffic.

Outside the car I saw the roses. In a split un-thought second I turned my car out of the traffic, ignoring the beeping and squeaking of tyres from behind and entered the Adelaide Botanical Gardens.

At the parking meter I shook my purse as if that would help coins to magically appear. Should I take a small risk?

'Smell the roses.' Closing my purse I walked towards the entrance. I was going to prove to Mum, really to myself, that I could be spontaneous and take a risk. But my mind churned in protest. By stopping I might get a parking ticket and I would be late for the meeting. For the first time in years, Garnet's technology was put on hold as I walked into the rose garden.

A blond haired man stood on the path inside the entrance. He's cute, I thought. His smile was welcoming. I smiled back, his blue eyes clear like precious gems. I kept walking wondering if I should've tried to start up a conversation.

'Daddy, daddy, I've found Mum's roses.'

Well maybe that's why I'd kept walking, he was married. I scratched him from my mind as I took a deep breath and smelled the air which was thick with sweetness. Leaning forward over the pink opened rose I took another breath. The scent was delicious. I moved to the next open rose on the bush and took another deep breath. Something wriggled in my nose and I automatically sneezed. This was why I didn't smell roses – bugs.

The man tried to suppress a laugh as he walked past holding his daughter's hand. Who would've thought I'd need practise at smelling the roses?

Determined to do this simple task, I moved to the white roses nearby. The late afternoon breeze played with the edges of the soft material of my dress. I felt the stress of the day blow away.

'Oh no!' The sound of tearing threads and a tug made me stop. I was caught in the thorns. Bending down I tried to free the delicate top layer of my favourite dress. My fingers worked away but they made the knot worse. There was no other choice; my dress would have to be sacrificed. This was going to be the last time I bothered to stop and smell the roses.

'Here let me help,' said the man. His daughter was further along the row of roses, playing her own game.

'How could such a beauty have thorns?' His voice was musical. His hand brushed mine away as he patiently began to untangle my dress. All I could do was stand and wait in close proximity of this hunky stranger. His masculine smell enhanced in the afternoon sun and sugared by the scent of the roses. My mind clouded with unfamiliar bliss.

'Which are your favourites?' God I sounded stupid. I was so out of practise, besides he was married – but my dress covered his fingers and I couldn't see if he wore a ring.

'The garnet coloured roses here which have caught you. They show the deep colour of passion and commitment.' Our eyes met and he winked. Immediately my cheeks increased in temperature.

'These are Mum's favourite,' said the girl holding a yellow bud.

'You shouldn't really pick them.' I couldn't believe I'd just said that! What was wrong with me? I wished he'd hurry up. I felt the warmth rise in my body, but this heat was unpleasant.

'Sorry.' I added. I was going to go home and make a commitment to celibacy. No, I had to do more. Maybe a self-imposed isolation would save myself from acting like a total idiot.

'Here, I'll just rip it.' I said unable to bear the tension of standing next to this man any longer. Besides, the delicate pastel pink material had ripped.

'No,' said the man and his daughter together. I felt truly trapped. If only he didn't look so...desirable.

'Nearly done. The rose is for Mum isn't Haley.'

'Mum would smell these the most before she died.' The girl pressed the rose to her nose.

'Oh, I'm sorry.' I felt another wave of uncomfortable heat reach my cheeks. There would be no way this man would ever be interested in someone like me who said stupid things and couldn't even smell a rose without becoming entangled in its thorns. I didn't notice he'd freed my skirt.

'Oh it's ruined.' He held the material and looked at the tiny holes.

'I can buy another.' Not that I needed an excuse to go shopping.

He swiftly picked a garnet coloured rose bud and winced as a thorn pierced his skin.

'We come here each week, at this time,' he said as he gave the rose bud to me. His finger bled a little.

'Here.' I took out a lavender scented tissue from my bag and wrapped his finger.

'Now we are even,' I said.

'I hope not.' He sounded disappointed or maybe I was dreaming, intoxicated from being so close to him. Why would he want me? I was stressed and uptight at the best of times.

'I'm Andy.'

This was too much. I had only stopped to smell the roses and not too talk to a man. A man whose looks and gentleness made me want to consider him. I turned and ran away, too scared to trust myself to stay.

* * *

The rose sat on my desk at work. Each day I would smell the rose, many times. And remember I'd been too scared to tell him my name or even to say thank you. How could I find the courage to go to the garden again?

The following Thursday I left work early. To make sure I had enough time to do more than smell the roses.

I found it hard to breathe as I parked my car. The air conditioning was now fixed, but I was still sweating. Would Andy be there? I wore my new dress, a light blue floral design with a tight waist and flowing skirt, with no soft outer layer to snag on thorns.

Fumbling coins into the parking machine I struggled to keep my hands from shaking. I felt torn. Part of me wanted to see Andy, and an opposing part wanted to run again. With uncertainty I walked towards the roses. But Andy wasn't there.

Easy come, easy go I thought. 'Smell the roses.' Mum's voice echoed once more in my head. With nothing else to do, I began smelling the open flowers. Naturally checking each one first, to ensure there were no insects.

'Hello again.' Andy's soft voice surprised me.

'Hi.' I stammered back.

'Keeping your dress away from thorns?'

'Yes. Are you keeping your finger away from thorns?' I smiled back at him as he laughed. Andy held out another garnet rose bud for me.

'Thank you. I'm Jenny.' I said taking the rose.

'Jenny, I'm glad to see you again. Would you like to smell the roses with me?'

'Sure.' He took my hand and led me to another bush. I

felt my face redden with heat, the type of warmth that was enjoyable.

Taking a deep breath I felt the sweetness fill my body. There were no insects, and no thorns caught in my dress and there was a desirable man beside me. I felt myself relax in his presence as we moved between the bushes. Stopping and smelling, together.

'Daddy, come and kiss Mum's roses.' Hayley stood by the yellow rose bush waiting.

Andy walked over to his daughter and they smelt the roses.

'Do you want to kiss the roses too?' Hayley asked me. I felt like I was imposing on their family, but Andy signalled for me to come over. The three of us stood with our noses in the petals.

'Daddy I'm hungry.'

'OK let's go.' Andy turned to me. 'Next Thursday?'

'I'll look forward to it.' He moved closer and gave me a kiss. I felt my lips open and greet the intimacy with a new found confidence.

* * *

There were many rose buds on my desk. Not that I needed any more reminders or encouragement. I could barely wait until Thursday when I would see Andy again.

After the third meeting at the rose garden we had coffee and exchanged numbers. We met on the following Saturday for dinner, then again on Thursday at the rose garden.

Our relationship was like the garnet coloured rose buds he'd given me, ready to burst open with passion and commitment.

We kept meeting at the rose garden each Thursday. When we walked back to the cars, holding hands, I thanked mum for reminding me to stop and smell the roses.

11
LOSING THE PAST
Patricia Maw

By mid-morning the beach has begun to fill up. I open up the shutters on the front of the café and set out the tables and chairs. Far off, at the other end of the beach, a solitary figure saunters along the shoreline, sunlight glinting on his blond hair. I stretch my arms above my head and watch for a while before he disappears round the edge of the rocks. Then I go inside and switch on the urn before the rush starts.

It's always like this on sunny weekends out of season. People come from miles around with their chisels and hammers and bags to put their finds in. I don't know if there's a collective name for fossil hunters but whether they're eight or eighty they all have the same intent expressions and the same excited squeals when they've uncovered another ammonite.

Jack used to scoff on the rare occasions he came down to the beach. 'Look at them, Jess. All those people wasting time, going along with their eyes on the ground. They want to look up, look at the cliffs, they're perfect for climbing. I could teach them a thing or two.'

I'd never thought of fossil hunting as a waste of time. I suppose it's because I've grown up with it. It's something families do together round here and because Dad is the only family I've got I liked the idea of that. Dad bought the Rock Café after he took early retirement. 'It'll give me something to do,' he'd said. 'Keep me out of mischief.'

'It's not really viable, Jess.' Jack kept telling me. 'It needs updating. Bringing into the 21st century. People want café latte these days not instant. Perhaps I should have a word with your father. Put him straight.'

'Viable' was one of Jack's words. Along with 'progressive' and 'seize the moment'. I didn't think Dad would be very impressed by any of Jack's ideas but that was in the early days when I was in love.

'You're mad,' my best friend Angie had said scathingly. 'Jack Curtis, of all people! Honestly, Jess. He makes a career out of breaking hearts.' But I'd refused to listen. You know what it's like at the start of a new relationship. You don't want to hear anything bad about the person you love. And I thought I loved Jack.

He was everything I wasn't. Vibrant, imaginative, go-ahead. Or so I thought. But, sometimes, I had a strange feeling that we were in a race together, with Jack always several strides ahead of me and however fast I ran I was never going to catch up.

A carroty head appears over the shelf at the front of the cafe window, followed by a snub nose covered in freckles. 'Look what I found, Miss.' He holds out a grubby hand and slowly opens his fingers.

'Hello, Callum.' I take the small piece of rock from his palm and trace the spiral remains of the ammonite. They're ten a penny on the beach after a high tide but Callum's happy. He's in my Year Two class at the local school and he comes here most Sundays with his family. 'It's lovely,' I say, handing it back. 'Did you know it's over a hundred million years old?'

His eyes widen. 'A million trillion,' he shouts and runs, laughing, back along the beach.

Time doesn't mean very much when you're Callum's age, but this past year has seemed like an eternity to me. Jack had great ideas for the future. 'Leisure activities, Jess. Now there's a viable proposition.' He had it all planned. 'An Adventure School. That's what we'll start. Sailing, canoeing, rock-climbing...' His eyes shone. In his mind it was already a reality. He never understood that I had a job. One I enjoyed. One I was good at.

'Where does he think the money's coming from?' was Dad's only comment when I told him about Jack's plans.

'Jack says the Bank will give him a loan. He's working on a business plan...' but as I spoke the words aloud I wondered if they were as hare-brained as all Jack's other ideas.

'It doesn't do to get too carried away, Jessie,' was Dad's only comment as he puffed on his pipe and looked out of the café window at the distant horizon.

I wrap cling-film round the sandwiches and rolls and put some pasties to warm up. They'll be coming for their lunch soon. Those that haven't brought a picnic with them. I've been looking after the café on my own since Dad went to New Zealand to visit his sister. He's been promising to go for years but I think he felt now was a good time. He didn't come out and say so. Dad's not one for emotional pronouncements, but I knew he was worried about me. I went to pieces a bit after Jack's accident. I blamed myself even though I wasn't there when it happened.

We'd had another argument. Not that you could really argue with Jack. He never listened to what he didn't want to hear because he thought he was always right. He was going on a rock climbing course and he wanted me to go with him. But I didn't want to spend my weekend halfway up a cliff. I'm terrified of heights. Just looking at the cliffs here makes me feel dizzy. 'You'll love it, Jess,' he kept saying. 'Once you've got the hang of it,' he'd laughed. 'No pun intended. The secret is not to look down.'

'No, I won't love it,' I said. 'If you don't know that, then you don't know me very well. Why won't you listen to me?' That's the last memory I have of him. His crestfallen expression as I walked away.

They've started to come for their sandwiches now and I'm too busy to think about anything except pouring the next mug to tea. This is what Dad wanted, I suppose. Something to keep me occupied at weekends. To stop me feeling guilty.

'It was an accident, Jess,' he told me over and over again. 'The rope slipped. You couldn't have prevented it even if you'd been there.' I know he's right, just as I know now that Jack wasn't right for me. I like to have my feet firmly on the ground, while Jack…well, he always had his head in the clouds. I haven't told Dad this yet, but I was planning to end it anyway. Closure. That's what Jack would have called it. Only I didn't get the chance. The chance to say I was sorry.

The sun has started to sink behind the cliffs and most of the beach is in shadow. People are beginning to drift away; the last fossil has been unearthed, the last ice-cream eaten. Overhead the gulls are wheeling and screeching, looking for scraps. I clear away the debris, wipe down the chairs and tables and stack them in the lean-to shed beside the cafe.

In the distance I can see the lone figure again. He's walking towards me now along the edge of the beach, eyes cast firmly downwards. I put the last mug to drain, switch off the urn and run a comb through my hair. As he gets closer my breathing quickens and little tingles of anticipation run up and down my spine. I want him to hurry up, not stroll along as though he's got nothing better to do. I've never felt like this before, not even with Jack. In fact, never with Jack. He made me feel that, however hard I tried, I never measured up to his expectations.

I lock the café door and wait outside. This relationship is still in its early stages and we're both feeling our way, taking it slowly. But that's okay because I don't want to be swept off my feet again. Like Dad says, 'it doesn't do to get too carried away.' Anyway, I don't believe William is the carrying away sort. He's the science teacher at the same school where I teach history. He's steady, reliable, a bit like me. I know that makes him sound boring but he's not. He's got a quirky sense of humour, he makes me laugh and I'm happy when we're together.

'Hello, Jessica. Look what I've found.' He takes my hand and tips a cascade of tiny shells onto my palm.

'Tiger scallops,' I say, marvelling at their fragility, their pastel shades of pinks and yellows and greens. How does he know I much prefer shells to fossils? 'They're beautiful,' I murmur.

'Just like you,' he whispers in my ear and I forget everything else as he takes me in his arms and lifts me, ever so gently, off my feet.

12

SAM SOMETHING
Kate Blackadder

I know I shouldn't have listened, but they were talking rather loudly. And I'm nosey, of course. I have to be. I'm a journalist, always on the lookout for the big story. Although this conversation didn't sound like front-page news. A tale of mis-matched lovers, of betrayal ... more like the problem page.

I'd arranged to meet Big Jim, the paper's photographer, outside that new café in the square. I had time to kill so I went in and ordered a cappuccino. The only bad thing about a good cappuccino is that it takes ages to make so I stood at the counter with nothing better to do than look at myself in the mirror behind it.

I was wearing the shirt in trendy lime green that my ex-girlfriend Gina had chosen – before she was my ex-girlfriend that is. She said it sharpened up my image. I think it makes me look peaky and I don't know that I want, or need, my image sharpened but I know how much I paid for it so I won't be buying another one for a while. Gina wouldn't have approved of the tie though, blue with yellow sheep, a birthday present from my little niece. It would have been straight off to the charity shop if Gina were still around to see it. I raised my eyebrows and gave myself a rueful grin and got raised eyebrows and a rueful grin back – and a broad smile from the Italian mama who was setting out cakes.

'You want a cake? A pastry? Very fresh. Very nice.'

I shook my head automatically, forgetting that Gina was no longer around to remind me of the twin evils of butter and sugar.

Mama went on with what she was doing. 'You let me know if you change your mind.'

When I looked in the mirror again I saw two girls coming in. One of them sat down and the other came and stood behind me. She was very pretty with lots of wavy brown hair tied back with a ribbon.

'Kirsty,' she called to her friend – or perhaps her sister, they looked very alike – 'do you want anything to eat?'

Kirsty shook her head. She had brown curly hair too but hers hung loose.

'Just the coffee, thanks, Carrie.'

I was just wondering if I could remember any of my pre-Gina chat-up lines when I was handed my cappuccino and had to decide whether to have chocolate or nutmeg on it. As I sat drinking it – and wishing I'd chosen chocolate – I listened idly to the girls' conversation. Kirsty's recent wedding; their Mum and Dad – ah, so I was right, they were sisters; work, Kirsty's boss Gina who'd just ditched her boyfriend and resigned from her job …

Gina! Did they mean my Gina, my ex-Gina? It's not a very common name.

'I thought she was madly in love with what's-his-name – she showed me his photo once when I went in to meet you at the office. He looked sweet,' said Carrie.

Sweet! I sat up straight and frowned at my cup, trying to look as unsweet as possible, in case it really was me she was talking about.

I soon found out.

'What was his name anyway?' asked Carrie.

'Something short – Brad, Leo – no, it was Sam. Sam… Something,' replied Kirsty. 'He's a journalist. Can't remember his second name.'

That's me – Sam Something, Journalist. Recently chucked boyfriend of Gina Graham, Advertising Executive (and blue-eyed, long-legged blonde).

'He was a really good cook,' continued Kirsty. 'Gina said he would never let her near his kitchen.'

Almost true. For someone who was otherwise Superwoman she couldn't tell pasta from pesto. But I don't remember her ever offering to load the dishwasher.

'So what was the problem?' Carrie asked. 'He sounds perfect.'

You sound pretty perfect yourself, Carrie.

'Oh, he wanted them to settle down and have babies, according to Gina. You should have heard the way she said it. Babies! As if they were some alien species. And she moaned that he was always dragging her out on Sunday afternoons to look at family houses. She said she might think about moving in with him but only if they bought one of those penthouse flats – you know, the new ones down by the river.'

A slight exaggeration. She would only come with me twice to look at houses. The old vicarage – great potential for a vegetable garden, and the semi-detached near the station. I loved that semi. It had a great kitchen – state-of-the-art combination cooker, American fridge, the lot.

My mind must have been semi-detached as far as Gina was concerned. Why couldn't she have explained her views on domesticity instead of sending me a postcard from Ibiza telling me she was moving there permanently and she didn't think we should see each other anymore?

She'd made her point. An island in the Mediterranean is hardly handy for dropping in of an evening.

I finished my coffee but I didn't want to leave in case there were going to be more revelations about my private life.

I ordered another cappuccino – with chocolate – and an apricot pastry to keep Mama happy. I put them on my table and went back up to the counter to get a fork. On my way back I tried to look at Carrie out of the corner of my eye and had time to see she wasn't wearing a ring on her left hand before I tripped over her handbag and fell flat on my face. The fork clattered off into a corner.

Carrie jumped up full of apologies, which was nice of her since it wasn't her fault, and helped me pick myself off the floor. When we'd established that nothing was broken and I'd said something corny about men falling for her, I looked at her properly. She had warm hazel eyes and a wide smile. Then I remembered that she'd seen my photograph and I didn't want her to recognise me as poor old thrown-over Sam even if she did think I looked sweet. So I said I was fine, yes, I was quite sure and I went and got another fork, sat down again and stabbed the apricot rather viciously.

Not wearing a ring didn't mean anything of course. For all I knew she might be madly in love with some very rich, good-looking stockbroker and they lived together in unwedded bliss, in the semi-detached house by the station, and she was a stockbroker too and they travelled up to the city together every day on the train, and met for lunch in expense account restaurants, and sent each other erotic emails. And she was lovely to his little niece, and never threw out his ties, and never gave him lectures on what he ate, or told him that he should be more assertive about getting promotion.

Or maybe she lived in the old vicarage with a rich, good-looking artist, and wore floral wellies and grew unusual salad greens and three varieties of strawberries, and had just found out that she was expecting their first baby.

And maybe I should take up writing romantic novels.

Behind me I could hear the girls getting up to go and I heaved a sigh for what might have been.

The door opened and I thought they were leaving but it was someone else coming in.

'Kirsty! Carrie!'

I recognised that voice. Big Jim always shouted. He thought it made him sound taller. Should I try and hide under the table? Make a break for the gents? No, too late.

'Sam!' It was my turn now. There was no escape. I got up, wiped the cappuccino froth from my mouth, and went over.

There he was, kissing the girls – pushing the camera round his neck to one side and standing on tiptoe – and exclaiming how lovely it was to see them. He held out an arm to include me in this happy reunion.

'Kirsty and Carrie, used to live next door to me when they were nippers. Couple of crackers now, eh Sam? Girls, this is Sam ...'

I held out my hand.

'That's Sam Something, journalist,' I said, 'don't they say listeners hear no good of themselves?'

Big Jim was looking quizzical and the girls were obviously struggling to decide whether I was upset or not.

I started to laugh and the girls joined in, looking relieved.

Carrie's hand was warm in mine and her eyes were

dancing. She may have been laughing at my tie but I don't think so. The way she was looking at me – well, somehow I didn't think there was a stockbroker or an artist or anyone else waiting for her at home.

And of course she knew that Sam Something was currently very free and available.

No, this story is not for the problem page, and definitely not for the lonely hearts.

Maybe, one day, for the engagements column?

13
CELEBRITY KENNELS
Gill McKinlay

"I'm sick of television," Jenny said. "There must be more to life than watching Celebrity Kennels."

Jenny's husband Kevin disagreed. He loved Celebrity Kennels, a reality TV programme where fifteen dogs of the rich and famous were housed together in a huge custom-built kennel to see how they all got on.

"Why not go out with Rose," Kevin suggested, as he eagerly awaited the latest canine eviction. "You haven't seen her in ages."

It was true. Jenny hadn't seen Rose for months, mainly because Rose never went anywhere in case she missed an episode of Corrie.

But Jenny had other ideas.

"Why don't we do something together for a change?" she asked.

"We could, but if you went out with Rose, I could watch the football in peace. I know how much you hate it."

So Jenny phoned her mate and they arranged to go for a drink in The Snail and Whippet.

They didn't get out until late. Rose had watched all the soaps first. Then they fought their way through a three-deep throng of blokes to get to the bar, "We're the only females in here," Jenny said.

"The football's on…"

Wedged into a dimly lit corner, surrounded by

shouting fans, it wasn't long before Rose developed a splitting headache.

"I think I'd better go."

"What about finding somewhere a bit quieter?" Jenny couldn't face going home to a poodle barking its head off in the diary room.

"Not worth it," Rose downed her mineral water and picked up her bag. "The pubs will all be showing the football but there's a good film on later. If we leave now, we'll just catch the start."

The film obviously didn't appeal to Kevin. Jenny arrived home to find him slumped in front of Paws for Thought, a CK spin-off featuring the latest evicted dog and its sobbing owner.

"These programmes get more and more ridiculous," she moaned. "I'm off to bed."

Next day, Jenny phoned Rose.

"How's your headache?" she asked.

"Gone," Rose replied.

"Good. How about we go for a meal one night so we can have a proper gossip?"

"Why don't you come round here?" Rose suggested. "Roy's away so we could have a girlie night in."

Jenny went shopping for the occasion.

"Ooh lovely." Rose shoved the wine in the fridge. "It can be chilling while we watch Emmerdale and eat these chocolates."

"And then she found Only Fools and Horses on a cable channel followed by Casualty," Jenny complained to Kevin when she got back. "Why is everyone so obsessed with telly?"

"Dunno love." Kevin was glued to the screen. Celebrity Kennels had reached its penultimate episode.

Would it be the terrier-in-a-handbag or the dopey Afghan hound that left the kennel? Kevin's money was on the Afghan. He'd developed a bit of a thing for mans' best friend since the show had started.

"The terrier belongs to that woman from Holby City," he explained. "He's the odds-on favourite to win the show."

Jenny couldn't have cared less. She left Kevin to it and went for an early bath.

Wandering around the library the following day, Jenny found the answer to her prayers. Literary Discussion Group, she read off a poster on the wall. Chat and Make New Friends.

There was a meeting that night.

"Hello." The group leader collared her the minute she walked through the door. "I'm Cheryl." She introduced Jenny to three other women. "It's the finale of Celebrity Kennels tonight so that's probably why we're a bit thin on the ground. I've taped it to watch later," she added.

Cheryl then asked if anyone had watched the recent repeats of Pride and Prejudice.

"I thought we could analyse Colin Firth's portrayal of Mr Darcy." Cheryl said.

"I haven't even read the book," one woman admitted.

"Me neither," Jenny said feeling somewhat ashamed. "Let's read it before the next meeting."

Cheryl gave her an odd look.

"My original idea was to discuss classic literature that had been made into television dramas. I'd also planned for us to go to the cinema to see some big screen adaptations…"

For the rest of the evening, the talk turned to Bridget Jones's Diary and the burning question of whether Colin

Firth was more fancied than Hugh Grant. It was obvious that Cheryl had a bit of a thing for the delectable Mr Firth, and although Jenny wasn't immune to his charms, the group wasn't quite how she'd imagined it.

Back home, Celebrity Kennels was over. The terrier had won a lucrative contract advertising dog food.

"They're going to make another series, though," Kevin told her "I can't wait for it to start."

Jenny rolled her eyes.

"You really should get out more," she told Kevin. "Why don't we get a dog and then you'd have to walk it…"

Jenny was amazed it hadn't occurred to either of them before.

So they sat side by side on the sofa and made plans. It was the closest they'd been in months.

"We'll take the dog for some long walks together at the weekends." Jenny said as she snuggled closer. "But you'll have to walk it during the week."

She knew Kevin would only walk as far as the pub. But the landlord wouldn't mind a dog sitting under the bar and he could watch the big screen while downing a pint. At least it would get him out of the house.

The following day, they visited the local rescue centre.

"This mongrel is a lovely creature." The woman in charge told them, "So friendly. He's ideal for first time owners."

The dog looked up at Jenny and Kevin with huge doleful eyes. Jenny stooped to stroke his soft brown fur. He was perfect and she was in love with him already.

"He's called K9," the woman went on. "You know, from Doctor Who. He won't be any trouble and he loves watching telly…"

14
SOMETHING TO MOVE YOU
Alice Parrant

As Molly approached the red brick building, she took a moment for herself, before walking to the front door. The breeze against her face caressed her hair. It felt like so long since anyone had held her. Somewhere nearby a blackbird was singing. She paused for a while, listening to its sweet song.

It had been a day very like today that she had first spoken to Frank. He had accidently kicked a football straight into her, leaving a large damp stain in the middle of her dress. She remembered how her cheeks had glowed when he ran over in concern.

A few years her senior, Frank had seemed far too sophisticated to talk to Molly. Yet after the football episode, he always smiled when he saw her in the village. It wasn't until she turned twenty and was working in the town nearby that he called to ask if she would like to go out to the cinema. The rest just fell into place.

Molly pressed the doorbell and heard its chiming tune resonate through the hallway. She looked at the plaque on the wall: 'Primrose Lodge'. The name made her think of a cosy countryside retreat by a quiet lake, where wild primroses might hide in the hedgerows nearby. She imagined majestic trees, high hills and wisps of wood smoke in clean, rural air.

This Primrose Lodge stood in a suburban street,

without a primrose in sight. The floors were covered in a hard, clinical lino and the corridors smelt of school dinners. Monet and Renoir dotted the walls, as well as some photos of a Christmas party. Molly did not recognise anyone in them and suspected they had been taken a long time ago.

"How is he?" she asked the uniformed assistant who came to the door.

"Doing well, Mrs Pearson. He ate all his lunch and painted a beautiful picture."

A beautiful picture! Molly thought of the muddle of blobs and smudges Frank usually produced. 'Probably looks like something Ben might have done when he was tiny,' she thought, as she pictured their teenage grandson. Frank had never been very interested in art, and it seemed rather silly to be encouraging this hobby so late in life.

Their shared passion had always been to dance. Having reached county level in ballroom, they had been pretty good.

Molly allowed her memory to take her back to those competitions and the rush of nerves and anticipation as they waited for the results. What was life without something to move, delight and motivate you? Becoming rather addicted, she had tried salsa, flamenco, tap and even took up belly dancing in her sixties. The fluid movement in her hips and finding her own type of wiggle made her feel new, alive and wonderfully attractive. Frank had watched entranced as she practised in front of the mirror.

"Who says old married couples don't have any fun?" she'd giggled falling into his arms.

Molly felt her handbag drag on her shoulder. She didn't feel old, not really, but belly dancing seemed like such a long time ago. Part of another life.

It had started small as these things usually do. Senior moments. Frank just seemed to have more of them than other people. She'd spied him watering a cactus and putting his reading glasses into empty coffee mugs. It was when he got lost on his way home from the garden centre and announced one afternoon that he'd better go and pick the girls up from school that Molly began to worry.

"I've told you before that I don't want to buy anything," Frank was sitting by the bay window in his bedroom in a flowery, upholstered armchair.

"Darling, it's me, it's Molly," she said as brightly as she could. For some months now, Frank hadn't recognised her. Often, he thought she was a member of staff but this salesperson thing was new. He had always disliked cold callers.

"How are you?" She sat down beside him.

"Can't complain."

"That's good, love."

Molly reached into her handbag for an old photo of Ben on his tricycle. 'Shame he had to turn into a sulky teenager,' she thought rather wistfully as she remembered his joyful, toddler laughter and the smell of his newly washed curly hair.

"Who's that child?" Frank was leaning over.

"He's called Ben and he's our grandson," Molly smiled. She was grateful that her family were around to support her, even if she didn't see as much of them as she would have liked.

Frank's face turned into scowl.

"I've just told you that I don't want to buy anything. My parents will be coming soon to take me home. Go away."

In public, Molly was generally able to put up an imaginary shield, but today, she scurried out of the front door before anyone realised that she was crying. The one thing she wanted was a cuddle from her husband and he didn't know who she was.

On arriving home, Molly began a frantic session of 'DeClutz'. This involved turning out drawers, shelves, wardrobes and storage cupboards, then dumping unneeded items into bin bags destined for the local charity shop. It was a cathartic exercise and her head always felt clearer afterwards.

Of late, Molly had needed more 'DeClutz' sessions than usual. She had already made one trip back to the charity shop to try and buy back some of the more impulsive 'chuck outs'. Perhaps she could offer the service to her daughters, though Molly wasn't convinced that it would be gratefully received.

Having hauled open the drawers in the spare room, Molly was greeted by a jingle jangle noise as a mass of scarves and jewels tumbled out. 'So that's where they are,' she thought. Sparkle, glitter and vibrant colours along with a few cassette tapes filled the floor as Molly reacquainted herself with her old belly dancing kit. She picked up a golden hip scarf and sighed; it was designed to be shimmied into life, filling up rooms with laughter and delight.

Molly looked at the scarf and watched as its tiny bells and sequinned coins quivered slightly. She wasn't sure if it would still fit and tentatively tried it for size. Shrugging off her fleece, she turned herself around in front of the spare room mirror. How lovely the swish of the fabric felt on her hips as they gently started to rotate! Gaining in confidence, she tried out a few of the old moves. Yes, she was carrying a little extra, yes, her hips creaked slightly, but yes, she still had it in her. And it felt so good.

* * *

"Oh, I'm glad you're here," Frank looked up from his flowery chair. "My knee's giving me murder and my wife's ready to murder me. I need some painkillers."

"Your poor wife," replied Molly, remembering when Frank injured his knee in a dance contest some forty years ago. He had been an absolute nightmare. She reached into her handbag and found a tube of spearmints. "This should do the trick," she said, slipping one into his hand.

"Ah, you're an angel," he said happily, popping it into his mouth.

Molly was looking into her handbag once again. This time she took out a bright turquoise hip scarf, with silvery coins and bells sewn on. She wrapped it around her hips. Next, she produced a bracelet and carefully placed it around her wrist. It too was encrusted with coins which spread out over the front of her hand. The bracelet then wrapped itself into a ring around her middle finger. She took a moment to admire it, feeling all together transformed.

Signalling to the care assistant who was waiting by a stereo in the corner, Molly began to shimmy to the bright, Bollywood beat which had started to play. She wiggled her hips as she found her way into the dance. Any apprehension she might have felt, dissolved. She felt light, free and in touch with herself once again. It almost felt like the old days.

Molly looked up for a moment and watched how the light from the bay window had caught the shiny coins on her scarf and was sending dazzling orbs of light dancing around the room with them.

Molly risked a peep at Frank. He was staring at her in enchantment.

"My Moll," he whispered and all of a sudden he was on his feet with her and they began a unique kind of waltz with some free style thrown in.

15
PIER INTO THE FUTURE
Susan Jones

Bianca could see the bright lights of the pier twinkling in the night sky. It was cold for August: she wrapped her paisley scarf over her head, and tucked it into her plum velvet jacket. Walking briskly along the promenade, she practiced what she was going to say when she got there. He would be waiting by the fairground. They had discussed it over the phone. He wanted to meet up in the same place they'd met all those years earlier, planning the future together. Brighton Pier was busy tonight. Late holidaymakers drifting along, nothing to do except gaze into the closed gift shops. Madam Zelda was still open for palm readings. The dun kin doughnut stall had a queue of already obese customers waiting in line to fill up with more calories than they could ever work off before bedtime.

Bianca was preoccupied with her thoughts. It was over twenty years since she'd seen Gerry, up until a few months ago. Their daughter Lisa had always kept in touch with her dad. The divorce had been hasty. They had married too young. Gerry had wanted to travel. Bianca needed Lisa to have stability of childhood unlike herself, and to be brought up in England. The separation happened two years after her birth. It had been a battle over whether to live in Brighton or America. Gerry had followed his acting career which had taken him to first

America, then all around Europe. She had made her life in Brighton. Working hard, taking washing up jobs and cleaning work in the Victoria Hotel on the sea front.

When a lease become available ten years later, Bianca was given first chance to take it on. It was a gamble, but she was confident she could make a go of it. It was the work she had done all her life, so how would it go wrong?

Life without Gerry had been awful, but travelling with Lisa and making fresh starts every six months was the last thing Bianca wanted. All her life her parents had dragged her from one new school to another. She had no roots or childhood friends; it had left her with a feeling of being lost. There was no way in the world she wanted her daughter to go through the same. Bianca made sure she had a different kind of upbringing. Even at the cost of being a one parent family.

As years passed, Bianca came to realise that her stubbornness had cost her the man she loved. But seeing Lisa growing into a confident young woman who passed her driving test first time, got a job in Heathrow airport, and didn't think twice about boarding a plane to visit her dad, no matter where in the world he was, gave her the knowing feeling that she had taken the right choices staying and living in one place.

Lisa knew she was a Brighton girl born and bred, and not from a bit of everywhere as Bianca had always told people jokingly, being described as a 'Heinz 57 variety' got a bit boring after a while.

'Funny how we always want for our children the opposite of what we had ourselves,' she pondered. Maybe Lisa would jet around the globe with her family, and reverse the tables yet again. Would she have been the same outgoing, loveable, funny gregarious girl with loving parents, but travelling around? She would never know.

Bianca thought about Gerry often. Sometimes at weekends, when he'd had a drink, the phone would ring.

"Hi, it's me, how are you?" Bianca always made a point of saying,

"Hello." But then as soon as she could, she would shout Lisa to the phone. That was his reason for calling. After chatting to Lisa, and hearing her daughter saying,

"Yeah, yeah, yeah, o.k. bye, bye, bye," It always ended with.

"Mum, he wants a word with you." Half excited, and half annoyed, Bianca always took the phone. Gerry's soft, gentle voice spoke.

"I love you, Bianca." Oh, she couldn't afford to fall into his fantasy, but it was good to hear, so all she could say was.

"Good. Bye now." And replace the receiver. This occurred regularly, and without realising it, Bianca came to look forward to Gerry's calls, and the loving compliments that followed with, "I love you, Bianca." Each time they spoke.

It was when Gerry dropped Lisa back home after holidaying with him in America that she clapped eyes on him for the first time in years. He had insisted on coming in the taxi to make sure she'd got home safe. The same girl who had been completely capable of catching the plane which took her all the way across the Atlantic, and then taking a taxi to New York, and finding his apartment all on her own. But somehow Bianca was so glad he had.

She'd indulgently, slowly breathed in the image standing in front of her now. Taking in every inch of the man she'd married. Her Gerry, the man she'd fallen in love with all those years ago. Those eyes that had belonged only to her, those soft lips surrounding his mouth that had told her so many times that he loved her. His quiet, precise voice; gentle but so sure in his intentions. The world stood still while Gerry looked deep into her eyes, and held her close.

"You're looking good."

How was it that he could turn her to jelly with just three words?

Now, after phone calls that had gone on long into the night, butterflies in the stomach every time her text signal bleeped, here she was, on her way to meet him. The man she'd married when only eighteen, divorced in her twenties, and here mid-forties was off again.

It all felt extremely odd, she was that same girl of eighteen, yet she wasn't. Running the hotel had been hard work. Years of early mornings, late nights were wearing her down. She ached all over and her head buzzed with anticipation. What did she think would come of this meeting? Did she want him back? She couldn't think straight at this moment. After the brief meeting when Lisa came back from America, Gerry had knocked her off her feet. She had been ticking along nicely enough, but seeing him again after twenty years, just confirmed her feelings.

Entering the pier was no different than usual except now her heart was banging in her chest. She saw him before she got there, leaning on the rail. His silhouette outlined against the fading skyline. He stood alone looking out towards the sea. Nervously she tapped gently on his shoulder. He turned; she smelt a mingling of cigarettes combined with beer, warmth and always so much love. The unique smell that told her with eyes closed it was Gerry; one that she remembered from all those years ago. Living rough together, sleeping on the beach with just a sleeping bag for cover.

"Hi there."

"Bianca." She almost felt too nervous to look at him, when she did fireworks exploded inside her. She wanted him. She could see in those eyes that he felt exactly the same. She would have done anything for him when she was eighteen, except bring up their baby on the move. Her motherly instincts had won over her love for this man. She was forty two now, nothing had changed, except that now Lisa had her own life, and she was ready to start living hers. They kissed, slowly, gently at first. His mouth felt soft, tasted as though it belonged to her. For what felt like forever they hungrily made up for lost time. She knew from that moment they would be together forever. Music from the sugar babes filled the air. Gerry finally led Bianca to a nearby bench.

"I've been making plans to move back to England, Bianca." She was floating on air. "It's what I need to do."

"What are you missing, sea air, dunk kin doughnuts, our daughter?" Bianca eyed him teasingly.

"There's only one reason I want to come back, she's sitting by my side." Just for a moment time stood still. They held each other so close. Not needing any more words.

16

THE DECISION
Patricia Fawcett

'Does that mean you're not coming, Katherine?' Mom asked.

'Not absolutely,' I hedged, hearing the exasperation in her voice, sitting up straighter in my chair as if she could somehow see me. 'But it's very doubtful I'm going to get the time off.'

'Well, honey, it's just too bad of you,' she said, the rebuke loud and clear across the miles.

I sighed. I could picture her sitting on the porch in the house up in one of the New England states taking in the last of the afternoon sun. Cooling down a little now that September is here but still warm and pleasant no doubt and the porch at my childhood home is a particularly charming place to spend time. The house is very Huckleberry Finn complete with picket fence sitting amongst a block of similar white painted homes in the pretty little town that was home to me for the first eighteen years of my life.

No longer.

Home is now a small apartment in New York, a pretty good area in fact because I am scaling the heights rapidly in my job in finance. After I graduated I got a lucky break and Simpson Associates, who were willing to give me a chance, are soaring ahead taking me with them. Financial whiz-kid my dad calls me, telling anybody who cares to listen. He's so proud of both of us, me and my brother John.

It is only a quick hop on the plane up to Boston and dad always picks me up from the airport and drives me home but the way mom carries on sometimes you would think I lived on the other side of the world. What she really wants is for me to settle down with a nice man and have kids

She just doesn't understand how my mind or my job works.

'I have a meeting on Tuesday, an important meeting,' I told her now, trying to explain. 'I initiated it so it will look lousy if I don't turn up. If I can't make it we'll have to cancel and Joe hates to do that to clients. It shows lack of commitment,' I finished, hearing her sigh. 'Look, mom, I'm really sorry but I don't see how I can be there.'

'It is your grandmother's funeral,' she said in her quiet voice, the dangerous voice we used to quake at when we were young. 'How do you think it will look if we're not complete as a family? John is coming ...'

John lives in Seattle and his journey would be a lot more difficult than mine, but even if he had to cancel a hundred of his operations – he is a surgeon – he would still be there, at that cute wooden church in the pretty square supporting our parents and being seen by everybody to be a good son.

And that makes me the wicked daughter if I fail to turn up.

We ended the conversation a little tersely and I left things in the air telling my mother I would get back to her after I had spoken to my boss. Tossing the phone aside I could only guess at his reaction when and if I dared ask for time off. In our business taking a vacation is something other people do, less successful people, and at Simpson Associates we are expected to be there practically from dawn to dusk.

My grandmother was, or had been, such a sweet lady and as I waited for my ready meal to heat through, I felt tears welling up which I brushed away furiously. I do not cry prettily like some women. When I cry I look like nothing on earth ending up with a blotchy face, snotty nose and panda eyes to accompany the great hiccupping sobs. When I was little, it was often my grandmother who would console me after a bout of crying, putting her arms round me and stroking my hair until I calmed down.

'Blow your nose, sweetie-pie, and go and wash your face,' she would tell me before shooing me gently away. To me, even then she was like something out of the 'Little House on the Prairie' a real old-fashioned sort of grandmother. My mother is much more up to date, currently red-haired with a good layering of make-up and fantastic legs for her age.

I have the legs. But I'm more my dad's daughter in looks, muddy blonde and blue-eyed, not beautiful but if I seriously work at it I can pass as OK in candlelight and I have been told my smile is real special.

The gorgeous guy who told me that is real special too and that side of my life, the private side, is simmering nicely just now. I dare not mention Richard to mom because she'll have the wedding invitations ordered and be in a complete swoon when she hears that, in addition to being tall dark and handsome he is a graphic designer with his own company and travels regularly to the United Kingdom on business and has hinted at a vacation in Europe next year for the two of us. Vacation as in honeymoon maybe and even my boss Joe could not deny me time off for that. We are taking it slowly but I think we both know that it is the real thing.

My grandmother was in her eighties and her illness mercifully short so we must thank God for that. I recalled the last time I had seen her. She looked so little, seemed to have shrunk into herself, as she lay on her big bed, propped up on lace-edged pillows, her skin almost translucent but her eyes still bright. It was the height of summer and light flooded in through the window.

'Katherine, sweetie,' she said, as I took her hand. It felt so frail and I could feel the tears starting up as I remembered how vibrant she had been once upon a time, picking me up when I was small and twirling me around. The tables had turned for she looked so frail and was probably light as a feather now. 'I am so proud of you,' she went on. 'Your father's told me all about your wonderful job. Didn't I always tell you that you could do whatever you wanted if you put your mind to it? Don't take any notice of your mother. She never had any ambition whatsoever.'

'I love you,' I told her when I left her, feeling in my heart that it might be the last time I saw her. She felt like a bag of bones as I hugged her and because the tears were now very obvious I did not look back as I went out of the room because I did not want her to see me so upset.

My grandmother, of all the family, understood about my work and how important it was to me and I know she would forgive me for not attending her funeral. The phone call from my mother got to me though and next morning I found myself drifting past Joe's office several times wondering if I dare risk it. Commitment is the buzz word here and that means the job comes first. Joe has a long suffering wife and a couple of kids but I'm not entirely sure he remembers their names and he certainly has to be reminded of their birthdays.

'What the hell's the matter with you, Katherine?' he asked at last catching me as I sloped past. 'Something on your mind?'

'Well ...' I edged past and he waved me to a seat. Beyond his desk, behind the wide expanse of clear glass it was a glorious morning although you feel so isolated up here that the weather doesn't really exist unless it's blowing a gale when you could swear the whole beautiful building moves just a tad.

'Tell me,' he coaxed, glancing at his watch. 'You have five minutes.'

'It's my grandmother's funeral on Tuesday,' I told him. 'Back home. I really want to go.'

'Jesus!' He gave me one of those smiles of his that manage to be incredibly sinister. 'Grandmother's funeral, eh?'

'Yes,' I snapped. 'And if you think I'm making it up, Joe, would I do that? If I wanted time off to screw my boyfriend I'd tell you.'

He laughed. It's the language he understands and I've gotten used to it even though just saying those words made me cringe inside as if my mom or worse my grandmother herself was outside the door listening. Deep down, I am not that sort of foul-mouthed woman but in this game you have to act tough sometimes.

'Take the day off,' he said with a shrug. 'Cancel your meeting and rearrange it for the following week. Nothing lost.'

I could not believe it. 'Thanks, Joe.'

'Don't thank me. After all, Katherine, they are one of our major clients and I'm sure they will understand completely if we suddenly act like assholes. Off you go to your grandmother's funeral although …' his eyes narrowed and I looked away at the surrounding buildings that very nearly scraped the sky. 'She's dead. She won't know whether you are there or not, will she? And you can always sweeten your mother. Send her some flowers.'

I flinched at the brutal words. She was dead. My beautiful grandmother was dead and a little pain shot through me as I stood there trying to avoid eye contact with him. I was a wreck since I had heard the news but I didn't want to show any weakness, not in front of Joe. There was no need for him to spell it out. My job was on the line here. He had sacked people for less or made their lives so unbearable that they were forced to look elsewhere.

And yet. I thought about my grandmother and the rest of the family and how much small town life mattered to them and how it would matter to them if I was absent.

As for my job, I thought long and hard about that and it was no longer the dream job it had once been. The money was good, sure, but was that enough? What on earth did I want from life? Did I want a small town existence, the sort of thing Richard had hinted at? I gathered that he wanted to start afresh, move from New York, buy a house in some pretty little New England town, rather like my home town, somewhere clean and wholesome to bring up the kids he wanted.

But was his dream mine? And would I be satisfied with that?

He kept asking questions about my career and at first I had been flattered, going into details, letting him know that I was pretty important, made some tough decisions, working on paper with a million dollars most days.

What he wanted was for me to say I was willing to give the whole thing up for a future with him. And just now, I was not sure. I needed to talk to somebody, not my girlfriend but someone closer. Grandmother would have been the very best person. She would have understood, she would have given me the proper advice but she was gone.

In a flash, in my apartment that evening, I made the decision. I would go to the funeral and because my little car needed an airing I would drive up Monday after work even though it would take hours, spend the day with them and drive back on Tuesday evening so that at best I would only miss one day. I would be a zombie on Wednesday but at least I would gain a commitment point.

Keep the options open and I knew Joe would come round. After all I had seen him looking at my legs and knew that, although it was just a fantasy on his part and he would not cheat on his wife, he would hesitate about getting rid of me.

Sexist? You bet.

I knew he would still be at the office so I rang him there and then to tell him. I had to do it quickly before I got cold feet.

'No sweat,' he said coolly. 'I'll leave you to sweeten up the clients. Wear a short skirt when you see them.'

'Sure, Joe.'

Yes, it still went on even in the twenty first century.

Still as I told Richard later, omitting the bit about the short skirt of course, it was my grandmother's funeral and I would never forgive myself if I missed it. Had I done the right thing I asked him?

'Of course. I would have expected nothing less of you,' he said, taking me into his arms. 'There are some things that we just have to do. When you get back, darling, we'll have a special dinner together. There's something I want to ask you.'

'Oh really!' I teased him but he wouldn't say anything more although he did not need to. He told me he loved me instead and anyway I know a pre-proposal when I hear one.

Alone in bed that evening I thought of my grandmother. She might be puzzled by my decision, maybe even say that I had done the wrong thing but I knew I had not. And there was far more to it than that. It was not just a decision about going to a funeral or not, it was a life-changing decision because when I got back I was going to tell Joe to stuff the job. Small town life beckoned and it was looking cosier and more attractive by the minute.

I know it will cause a few problems in the office on the ninety-ninth floor of the World Trade Center in the heart of Manhattan but, honestly, when you get down to it, next Tuesday, September 11th, will be just another day.

17
A PAST LIFE
Susan Wright

Christopher didn't choose the best time to tell me he'd lived before. I was dashing around getting the living room ready for an angel party when he came downstairs in his cute doggy pyjamas and blurted out the words.

I stared at him in astonishment as he told me he could remember a woman who had been his mother before, and a tingle ran down my spine as he recalled living in a big red brick house, but there was furniture to move and nibbles to put out in the few minutes before Cassandra and my friends were due to arrive, so unfortunately I just didn't have the time to ask him any questions or listen any more.

I had to send him back up to his room and promise him faithfully that we'd talk about it some more in the morning.

Actually, I would have happily chatted to him about it again later that night, because I've always been fascinated by reincarnation and his words echoed in my mind all the time Cassandra was going on about her archangels and her white feathers, but Christopher was fast asleep by the time all my friends had gone, so I looked at his beautiful chubby face, pushed his dark hair out of his eyes and went to bed feeling impatient and excited.

I woke him up quarter of an hour earlier than usual the next morning so we would have time to talk. I sat down on his bed, called his name to wake him up and broached the subject before he'd even rubbed the sleep from his eyes.

"Do you remember your other mother's name?" I asked him.

"Yes," he nodded. "It was Sandra."

"Oh right," I said. "The same name as Nana. And what did this Sandra look like?"

"I don't know," Christopher shrugged. "Can't remember. She was tall and thin, I think. I can't remember her face or her hair or anything but she always used to smell nice…and she used to cuddle me all the time."

"Did she?" I smiled.

"Yes," Christopher nodded, his brown eyes looking wistful. "She did, but you don't cuddle me at all anymore, Mum."

"Oh, Christopher," I breathed, as my heart lurched in my chest. "I'm so sorry."

I felt awful. Because Christopher was right. I had stopped cuddling him. I'd stopped doing a lot of things since Mike had walked out. My world had fallen apart when my marriage had come to an end and I'd been so wrapped up in my own pain that I'd been blind to how much Christopher was hurting, but the look in his eyes and the sorrow in his voice really got to me right then so I moved across the bed, took my six year old son in my arms and held him really, really tight.

I breathed in the scent of his hair, felt his warmth against my face and became overwhelmed with my love for him as tears pricked in my eyes.

"I'm so sorry," I repeated. "I haven't been a very good mother just lately, have I? I'll try and do better, I promise."

"All right," Christopher gulped.

"I've been so selfish," I whispered, as I let him go and smiled into his eyes. "But this Sandra was a good mother to you, was she?"

"Yes, she was," Christopher nodded. "She used to take me down to the seaside. We played on the beach all the time."

"On the beach? Do you know where this beach was, Christopher? Do you remember?"

"Yes, it was in Brighton," Christopher replied without hesitation. "I lived in a big red brick house. Right by the sea. My name was Ashley and I had a dog... a big, black, shaggy dog."

"Did you?" I smiled, as I tried to visualise the dog. "Did he have a name?"

"Yes, it was Benjie," Christopher informed me.

"Benjie," I repeated. "That's nice. And do you know what your surname was when you were Ashley?"

"No, I don't," Christopher said, shaking his head, "but my other dad was called James, I think, and the house was right by the sea. It was big and red and..."

"Would you recognise it, Christopher?" I interrupted. "If we went there?"

"I think so."

"So would you like to go and try and find it? At the weekend?"

"Yes, I think so," my son said uncertainly, looking at me with his huge brown eyes. "Can Dad come with us, Mum?"

"Oh, I don't know about that," I said, doubtfully.

"I want him to come," Christopher insisted.

"OK," I said quietly. "I'll ask him."

But even as I spoke I felt pretty sure that Mike

wouldn't come. For one thing, he'd hardly been in touch with us since he'd left. He'd called round a couple of times to pick up some things and he'd taken to phoning me once a week to make sure that Christopher was all right, but our conversations always seemed to turn into arguments somehow and the last time we'd spoken I'd slammed down the phone.

I couldn't see that he'd want to spend any time with me and I didn't think he'd want to drag himself away from his girlfriend... especially once he found out the reason for our trip to Brighton, but Christopher was adamant that he wanted his father to come so once I'd taken him to school and done a bit of the housework, I looked at my watch and picked up the phone, feeling pretty certain that Mike wouldn't mind a quick call at work. I had no idea our conversation would take so long.

"Jenny," Mike said. "What's wrong? Is Christopher OK?"

"Yes, he's fine," I assured him. "But he wants to see you, Mike. He wants you to come with us to Brighton at the weekend."

"To Brighton? Why? What's at Brighton?"

"A big red brick house," I explained before taking a deep breath. "Christopher reckons he lived there in a previous life. He's been on this earth before, Mike!"

"Oh Jenny," Mike scoffed. "You've been filling his head with nonsense!"

"No, I haven't," I said. "I've never talked to him about reincarnation… or anything like that."

"Maybe not," Mike growled. "But you've talked about plenty of other weird things in front of him. Ghosts and aliens and such like! I told you before I left that you were going to upset him. Now he thinks he's been reincarnated, poor kid. He's not old enough to cope with these things, Jenny. I've told you that before. I don't know why you're so obsessed with all this weird stuff anyway. You're crazy! You're…"

"At least I'm here," I snapped. "Here for Christopher."

"Yeah, but you've gone really weird, Jenny," Mike said sadly. "Even before I went you were having crystal parties and mediums round and poor Christopher was being sent to his room. That's not still going on, is it?"

"No," I lied, the anger rising up inside me. "Anyway, I had to do something to fill the long, lonely evenings when you were supposedly working late!"

"You could have read," Mike suggested. "You could have played with…"

"Anyway," I interrupted, "we're getting off the subject. Are you going to come with us or not?"

"No, I don't think so…not for such a ridiculous thing."

"But it's not ridiculous, Mike," I said. "Christopher really remembers a past life."

"Yeah right," Mike said.

"And I've honestly never talked to him about reincarnation," I continued. "I don't even know much about it myself. I recorded a programme about it a few weeks ago but I haven't got round to watching it yet."

"Yeah, but I bet you've mentioned the subject in front of him. I bet you've talked about it with your friends."

"I haven't," I insisted. "He just came out with it, Mike. He reckons he lived in a big red house and he remembers his other mother and father. They were called Sandra and…"

"And what?" Mike asked.

"And James," I finished weakly.

"Oh, Sandra and James," Mike said, and I could

imagine the look on his face. "Funny your parents are called exactly the same thing, isn't it? You don't think Christopher is making all this up, do you? Just to get a bit of attention?"

"No, I don't," I said firmly, pushing any doubts to the back of my mind. "He says he was called Ashley and there's nobody in our family called that."

"No, but there's probably an Ashley at school and he's just weaving all these names into a story, Jenny. He knew you'd fall for it."

"He isn't," I snapped. "He said he had a big, black shaggy dog, Mike, and he says he'll recognise the house. We might be able to work out who he was! I know you don't want to come with us because you can't bear to be apart from your precious Anna for five minutes at a time but Christopher and I are going to Brighton on Saturday and he'll be really upset if you don't come."

"It's nothing to do with Anna," Mike muttered. "She and I are finished."

"Finished!" I cried as something lurched inside me. "But you've only known her a few months."

"Yes." Mike agreed sadly, "but she wasn't quite what I thought she was, Jenny, and... well, it's over, that's all. I made a mistake. I haven't phoned you to tell you because we only split up last night but I've been doing a lot of thinking since then and I shouldn't have walked out on you like I did. I'm sorry. I was wrong."

"Yeah, you were," I spat out, bitterness overwhelming me, "but you're only apologising because she's dumped you."

"No, I'm apologising because I want to come home. I miss you, Jen, and I miss Christopher too."

"Prove it then," I yelled down the phone. "Come with

us to Brighton!"

"OK," Mike said.

So Mike picked us up on the Saturday morning. He smiled weakly at me and gave Christopher a hug. He strapped our son in the car, sat in the driver's seat being very careful not to touch me and set off straightaway for Brighton. He didn't speak as we went along. He just concentrated on his driving. Christopher sat in the back looking out of the window for his big red brick house and I sat in the front gazing out of the windscreen and seeing nothing.

In some ways, it felt so right to have Mike beside me again. It reminded me of all the good times. It reminded me how much we'd been in love in the past. I glanced at his familiar profile, thought back over the early years of our relationship and wondered sadly how it all could have gone so wrong. I wondered too if I could ever forgive him. I blinked back the tears and thought about the lonely weeks we'd been apart, remembering with a pang of guilt how many times poor Christopher had been sent to his room, and then as I focused on the world outside and realised we were driving along the seafront, I turned round in my seat and smiled at my son.

"Have you seen your house yet?" I asked him.

"No," he replied shortly.

"Oh well," I said, "we've got a bit further to go yet."

"Not much further," Mike pointed out. "We're…"

"It might have been pulled down," I suggested. "The red house might not be here anymore. You don't know how long ago it was when you were Ashley, do you, Christopher? Was it a long time ago?"

"I don't know," Christopher mumbled.

He looked so sad. So worried. I smiled at him again

and turned back to look at Mike.

"It might have been pulled down," I repeated. "Or…"

"Or it might have been a figment of Christopher's imagination," Mike said quietly.

"No, I don't think so," I replied. "He…"

"Oh OK," Christopher yelled. "So I made it up!"

It turned out that Christopher had watched my programme about reincarnation. The little boy in the programme had remembered living in a big white house. He'd talked about his other family from the time he'd lived before and his mother in this life had been captivated by his every word so my little Christopher had made up a whole past life of his own so I would sit up and take notice.

He just wanted me to care.

There was no big red brick house. There had never been a black shaggy dog. Christopher didn't remember being anybody else. But he remembered how good it had been being him before his father had walked out and I guess he just wanted to feel loved and secure again, so Mike pulled over at the side of the road and I took Christopher in my arms and hugged him. For a long, long time. Then Mike cuddled him too. I looked at my husband as he held our son, our eyes met and all of a sudden there was that old familiar buzz between us. I couldn't help smiling. I couldn't help feeling a lot more positive about the future.

I could forgive him, I realised. I could learn to love him again – in time.

"I'm sorry," Christopher whispered, breaking into my thoughts.

"No, we're sorry," Mike said gently. "Your mother and I haven't been very good parents lately, have we? I'm not surprised you dreamed up another mother and father."

"And a big black shaggy dog called Benjie," I added, with a grin.

"Benjie?" Mike frowned.

"Yes, Benjie," Christopher nodded. "I saw a dog called Benjie on telly when I was sent to my room one night. He was lovely."

"Was he?" Mike asked, winking at me. "And would you like a dog of your own, Christopher?"

"Yes, I would," Christopher nodded enthusiastically, his eyes lighting up.

"Well, we'll have to see," Mike smiled. "I'm not making any promises, Christopher, because your mum and I need to talk about a lot of things but you might be able to have a dog. You've always wanted a dog too, haven't you, Jenny?"

"Yes, I have," I agreed. "Dogs are a lot of work though. You have to look after them all the time and you have to take them for walks. Long walks if they're big and black and shaggy."

"I can do that," Christopher shouted, his eyes sparkling.

"We can all do that," I said, looking at Mike.

Because if we were going to become a family again, it would be something we could all do together in the evenings.

18

DIAMOND TRAIL
Suzie Hindmarsh-Knights

Two kilometres away, on the dusty plain, a thin line of smoke caught Edward Peterson's eye. Through his binoculars, he watched it rise through a wall of dense shrub that followed a line, Edward guessed marked a section of the Cooper Creek.

It had been a few years since he'd last travelled this way. However, years of travelling through outback Australia, where he'd been searching to make his fortune in opal and diamonds now found him back. He'd travelled full circle; the lure of home was too strong to resist.

Edward kicked his stallion into a gallop. He was eager to see who was camped down by the creek. It had been many weeks since he'd sighted another human being. Travelling alone had its advantages. It had helped him through difficult times, but now he needed company.

He followed the meandering tree line, looking for a place to cross. The Creek was in flood, and as he surveyed the rushing water, he anticipated a difficult crossing. Impatiently he searched for a flattened part of the bank for easy entry into the water. He reined in his horse at the first opportunity, and dismounted to remove all his clothing and boots. Stowing them away in oilskins and securing them to the saddle, he re-mounted and urged the stallion down the embankment.

'Come on boy,' he spoke kindly to the stallion. 'A bit of water never hurt anyone.' The stallion crabbed along the edge of the bank unconvinced. Edward used the end of his rein in encouragement, and the stallion lunged outward and into the water.

They surfaced snorting water, and the stallion struggled to keep his head high, as he swam through the muddy water to the far bank. In the deepest part of the Creek, Edward swam alongside him, holding onto the saddle and only pulling himself back into it, moments before the stallion scrambled up the embankment, and shook the streaming water from his body.

Edward slipped from the saddle, drying himself before dressing and continuing towards the waft of smoke.

It was the time of the night, of deceptive light and dancing shadows, and by the time he reached the campsite darkness had stolen his vision. The fire was inviting, the ember's burnt blood red and hanging on a frame, a Billy can boiled.

He dismounted and looked around at the deserted camp. The crunch of dirt, and stones dislodged by cautious feet alerted the arrival of company.

'Put your hands above your head,' demanded a female voice. 'I won't hesitate to shoot you. I'm the local shooting champion. So don't do anything to encourage me.'

Edward raised his hands. 'I know that voice,' he said, swinging around.

'Stop, I never said you could move.'

The bullet passed within centimetres and Edward felt the air dislodged against his cheek. He stopped, not daring to take a further chance.

'Don't be smart mate, as I said, I'll use this. Now, what are you doing snooping around my camp?'

'I've been travelling for weeks and saw your fire. I could do with human company and a meal.'

'So you thought you could wander in without an invitation.'

'Are you a local?' Edward's cheeks dimpled as he smiled.

'What's it to you.'

'If you're who I think you are, I taught you everything you know. I only know of one other person, who can shoot that close without causing injury.'

'And who might that be?'

'Surely you can't have forgotten.'

The quietness of the night erupted with gutsy laughter. 'I'm done playing games mate. Tell me who you are?'

'It's been a few years, but I didn't think you'd ever forget me? Can I turn around Kate Fowler?

'Do I know you?'

'Under this beard and dirty clothing, yes I think you do.'

'Turn around slowly.' Kate stood with the rifle fixed to her shoulder. 'I said slowly.' She sighted him down the barrel. 'Edward?' Her arm dropped to her side as she stared across at him. 'Edward is that really you?'

'Yes Kate, I do believe it is.'

Kate stooped and carefully placed the rifle against the trunk of a eucalypt tree. 'Oh my God, Edward, I don't believe it.'

Edward caught her in his arms and swung her around in a circle. He breathed in her perfume and her familiar smell sent his heart racing. As he dropped her back to the ground, she beamed joyfully at him.

'Where have you been? I can't believe it's you. You do realise your parents have been frantic wondering what happened to you. Oh my God, I can't believe it. I need you to pinch me, so I know it's you.'

She barely took a breath in her excitement, and it buoyed Edward's spirit. 'It's been a long time. You look gorgeous.' He took her hand, and she pirouetted for him. Her long black hair feathered out behind her, and her skin glowed, while her blue eyes creased at the corners in laughter, she was a picture of health. He'd carried her image in his memory all these years, and it didn't do her justice.

'Why did you run away?' Her face lost its sparkle, as she cast him a solemn look.

'It's a long story.'

'Come and get warm by the campfire. I have all night.'

'First I need to take care of Diamond-Tina and more importantly take a bath.' Edward unsaddled the stallion and hobbled him in a patch of Creek grass. He removed his toiletries from his saddle bag and a change of clothes. Under the light of a new moon, he slid down to the water's edge and found a rock to sit on, where he could dangle his feet in the water. He worked through the weeks of beard with a razor and cut through the grime with soap. He felt like a new man by the time he rejoined Kate at the campfire.

She sat with a blanket wrapped around her shoulders sipping from a mug. 'You look like the Edward I used to know.' She smiled shyly at him. 'Want a coffee? It's strong but good.'

'Yes please.'

Edward accepted the enamel mug and dropped down next to her. He warmed his hands around the mug, blowing the steaming liquid and taste testing with the tip of his tongue. 'Kate, how are my folks?'

'Your father isn't well and hasn't been for some time. I don't think he's long for this world. After you left, he hit rock bottom.'

Edward thought about the fight with his old man on the night he'd walked out. They'd come to blows over his father's gambling addiction and the mounting bills. And if it hadn't been the quick thinking of his mother's concerned friends, they'd have been homeless. The homestead meant everything to his mother, it was her ancestral home. Just thinking about what his father put her through made his blood boil. Being the eldest he'd felt responsible and the need to find a well-paid job became paramount if he was to pay off his father's debts.

'And my mother?'

'Your mother's amazing. She's a battler and somehow manages to hold the family together. I guess you know your father re-mortgaged the family home. The banks were going to foreclose, but she managed to find enough money to pay another chunk of it.'

And that was because he'd followed through and sent funds. The mines paid well, and he'd made enough to live on and send surplus funds home. He knew by sending money to his mother; she would use it wisely.

'Aren't you going to ask about Joey?'

'Yeah, I was getting there. So how is my young brother?'

Kate stared at him over her mug and smiled. 'Joey hasn't changed. Your brother continues to breeze through life. He's charmed that one.'

'I know that better than most. Even so, when I left he had his eyes on you.'

Kate dropped her vision to the fire. The glow of the embers picked up the steely depth of her eyes. 'Why did you leave?' she whispered returning his gaze. 'I thought we had an understanding.'

What could he say? That he'd left because he caught his brother and his girl in more than an embrace. Because he could not be there and see the girl he loved taken by another man, especially when that man was his brother. And now he felt so overwhelmed by her presence, it was as though it happened only yesterday.

'Kate why are you out here alone?' The fire hissed as he upended the dregs of his coffee into the embers.

She shrugged further into the blanket. 'Chasing strays – you know how it is.'

He nodded before gazing up at the sky. 'Clouds are rolling in. Looks like the weather might change.'

'You haven't changed Edward Petersen. You can't avoid my question forever. However, you're right about the weather, I can smell the rain. Now it's time to get some sleep. Perhaps tomorrow you'll explain further.'

Edward knew she was upset with him. His silence was a barrier between them. Kate turned away and picked up her swag rolling it out next to the fire. She stepped into her sleeping bag pulling it under her chin, before wriggling her way under the canvas. 'Goodnight Edward.'

'Goodnight Kate.'

The wind arrived from the south in the middle of the night whipping along the Creek, fierce in strength. Edward lay watching the gentle movement of the swag on the far side of the cold fire. She opened her eyes and looked at him.

'I think we may need to make a move. It's going to pour any minute. There's a cattleman's hut not far from here.'

While Kate packed up camp, Edward saddled their horses. Kate lit the way with the beam from a torch. They rode a couple of kilometres along the Creek until Kate gestured towards a darkened hut.

Edward hobbled the horses and carried their gear inside. The smell of dust hit his nose.

'I think there's a kerosene lamp in the kitchen,' advised Kate.

The room brightened as Edward lit the lamp. 'The hut hasn't been used in a while by the looks. But it's better than being out in the weather.'

Edward rolled his sleeping bag a short distance from where Kate lay curled in hers. 'You never did answer my question about you and Joey?'

'Well you didn't answer mine?'

'What was the question?'

Kate lay propped on one elbow gazing at him. 'Oh sure - like you can't remember.'

'Okay truce. I had my reasons for leaving. Firstly, I needed to make money to get the family out of trouble. My mother was relying on me to fix things. The mines seemed like a good way of making big dollars. I tried my luck in Coober Pedy, then heard about the new diamond mine in New South Wales and decided to give it a go.' he paused before saying. 'And secondly, I thought you needed space from me.'

'Why on earth would you think that? Don't you realise how devastated I was? You left no note, no letters, nothing.'

'Kate, I'm sorry if I hurt you. But, it seemed like a good idea at the time.'

'I don't understand why you would say that. I loved you, and you left. That told me a lot about how little you cared about me.'

'I didn't leave because I didn't love you. I left because I thought you loved Joey.'

Kate sat upright. 'What are you talking about?'

Edward ran his hands across his face. 'How could you not remember? Kate, I saw you with Joey. The night I had that row with my father. I stormed away from the house towards the stables and you and Joey... well you were in a passionate embrace. He had his hands...'

'Yes I remember that evening very well,' interrupted Kate. 'I was upset that you and your father were fighting. Don't forget, I've seen how violent your father can get with a drink or two under his belt. Joey told me to wait with him. He was nice at first, reassuring me that you would be okay, and that you would sort everything out. He was trying to comfort me.'

'But you were kissing him, and he was...' Edward hated saying the words. 'He had his hands all over you.'

'You saw a kiss and yes he tried to touch me, but did you wait around to see me belt him across the face? Well, Edward, did you?'

Suddenly, Edward felt uncertain of what he'd seen that night. He remembered his father had come at him with fists raised, wanting a fight. He was drunk, and his mother was cowering on the couch, nursing a swollen eye. Edward remembered all of that very clearly. He had to protect his mother at all cost, so punches were thrown. His father had nearly got the upper hand, but Edward knocked him flat with a left hook under his chin. And then when he'd rushed out, he'd seen Joey and Kate.

'I've spoken to Joey a couple of times over the last couple of years, and he said you and him were an item.'

'When have you known Joey to tell the truth? I have

135

never loved and never will love Joey. He is the biggest pain in the ...'

A white flash of lightning lit the room, and a clap of thunder crashed overhead as the storm broke. The rain hit the tin roof, as Edward climbed out of his sleeping bag, and strode across to where Kate sat looking up at him. He dropped down beside her and reached to cradle her face in his hands. 'I'm sorry Kate.' He murmured, dropping his face into her hair and breathing in her familiar smell.

'You can't play with my emotions Edward Petersen.'

'I would never do that.'

'You left me damaged, broke my heart, and now you're back, you think you can take up where you left off.'

'Kate, could we start afresh, you know, start over?'

'I need to think about it.'

'At least you didn't say no,' he pushed up and returned to his sleeping bag and watched her snuggle down to sleep.

* * *

The morning was still, but for the dripping of raindrops from overhead trees onto the roof. Edward had slept little and now gazed on Kate's serene sleeping face and a deep feeling of love spread through him. He would do whatever needed to be done, to win back her affection.

She opened her eyes and slowly focused until returning his scrutiny. A smile spread across her mouth to her eyes and for many minutes, they stared at each other.

Edward thought about the years he'd thought she was lost to him. However, the reality was that she lay not that far away, she was no longer just in his dreams.

'What's your plan?' Kate broke the silence between them.

'I need to go home and make sure the family's okay.

I'm financially secure and want to purchase a place of my own. And I guess I need to speak to my brother.'

'Edward. Leave it. Don't worry about him.'

'But he needs to know the damage he's done.'

'He'll soon realise the deception is known.'

'Does that mean you're considering taking me back?'

'Perhaps,' she smiled.

He watched her stretch like a feline and stifle a yawn with her hand. 'While you consider that small problem, I'll give you another to ponder. Wait here.'

Edward climbed out of his sleeping bag and went in search of his saddle bags. He pushed his hand deep inside, and came out with a small velvet bag. He returned to Kate. 'I don't know why I hung onto this, when I thought you were spoken for. Nevertheless, I did and now I would like to give it to you. However, first I would like to ask you something.'

Kate looked at him in puzzlement. 'Ask me what?'

Edward gazed deeply into her eyes and twined his fingers tightly through hers. 'Kate Fowler, I love you. You are the only girl for me. I'm sorry I didn't talk to you on that terrible night. Will you find it in your heart to forgive me and consider becoming my wife?' Edward placed the pouch into her palm, closing her fingers around it. He stared into her eyes and wasn't happy with the years of emotion revealed to him. He had left her scared and unhappy and as he stared tears formed on her long lashes.

'I want to say yes. But, I need time,' she looked thoughtful then said. 'Let's start again and discuss marriage later.'

'Yes please.' Edward scooped her into his arms and covered her lips with his before she could object. He tasted the salty tears that streamed down her face. 'Are you unhappy?

'No, I'm very happy,' she sobbed. 'I love you Edward with all my heart. I just need to regain my faith in you.'

'I will never let you down again, I promise. Now please open the pouch.'

Kate pulled on the draw strings and tipped the contents into her hand. Shards of brilliant light sparkled back at her. 'Edward it's the most beautiful diamond I've ever seen.'

'When you're ready, we'll find a decent jeweller to set it.'

'It must be worth a fortune. It's too much.'

Edward pinched her lips together with his fingers. 'I worked long and hard to earn that Kate Fowler, so don't you dare to refuse it.'

'You continue to look after it. I will let you know when I'm ready for that visit.'

It was mid-morning before they finally emerged from the hut. The ground was washed clean from the rain, and the beauty of the morning left Edward feeling joyous.

On the highest point of the embankment, where the trees and foliage were dense and thick, there was a ledge that jutted out over the Creek. Edward led Kate to look at the beauty that was spread before them. As he stood holding her hand he felt a deep sense of wellbeing sweep over him. Part of his life's journey was now complete and the promise of a future with Kate by his side made going forward into the next chapter worthwhile.

19

THOSE PESKY KIDS
Maggie Jones

'Those pesky kids, they've done it again, Flo?' Bert shouted out to his long suffering wife. 'Did you hear what I just said?'

Flo chose to switch off from his moaning and groaning about their neighbour's children again, but suddenly he was standing right in front of her, repeating it all.

'I said, those pesky kids have been at it again, did you hear me?'

'Yes, I did.' She replied breathing in quickly, before slowly releasing it and shaking her head. 'I'm sure Fergus and Johnny are only being boys and letting off a little bit of steam. They don't mean any harm, Bert.'

At that he made a growling noise, before he turned away and went back outside again. She grabbed the mop and wiped the floor, removing his muddy footprints from it, tutting to herself. That was all he seemed to do lately, moan about the two boys. Always going on about how they've been at the bottom of his garden, and more importantly on his prized winning vegetable patch, nicking vegetables that he had painstakingly tended to over the last few months.

Flo knew Bert hated anyone touching anything of his, especially his vegetables. He'd nurtured them from tiny seedlings, and seen to their every need, until it was the time to pick them to eat, or for him to enter them in the local summer village show.

Sometimes, he could just be plain mean. Flo, couldn't see what was so wrong about the boys having a couple of carrots or the odd runner bean every now and again. It didn't hurt, she thought. They always had plenty enough to go around. Why, there was even a freezer full of his vegetable from last year still to get through, but as far as Bert was concerned, he'd grown them, and no one else was going to benefit from his hard work by eating them!

The worst thing had been when he'd gone round to see the boys mum, Becky Martin a few weeks ago. Bert had been hell bent on revenge. As far as he was concerned, the boys were nothing but thieves and criminals. Fergus was seven and Johnny just nine, but still he wanted his pound of flesh from them.

Flo had been in the sitting room with the window wide open. It had been a warm summer's evening, so she'd heard everything he'd shouted at the poor woman. He had really flown off the handle at her.

'You should learn to keep your boys under control. Do you know what they've gone and done now?'

Before Becky could attempt an answer, Bert continued with his rant.

'I'll tell you what they've gone and done. Not only have they stolen my vegetables from me in the past, but now they've gone and broken two of my panes of glass in my greenhouse.'

'But...'

'Don't you but me, my girl. I know what I know, and that was when I left my greenhouse last night, it was all fine and dandy, but today when I went down there to look at my carrots, there's all broken glass lying everywhere. No one else could have got into my garden to do it. It's your boys, and they are a menace.' He shouted.

'If I see them anywhere near my garden again, I shall call the police.' He raged at her, before turning around and striding down the path of her front garden, and slamming her gate for good measure, before going back indoors.

Flo heard Becky shout out, 'Bert, I'm sorry....' But by that time their front door was well and truly shut. She had felt awful at the way Bert had kept on at Becky; not giving the poor girl a chance to get a word in edgeways, it was terrible.

Back indoors, he had kept on and on about the two boys. He'd kept moaning, and when she tried to remind him of the times when he was a small boy and how he always took a sneaky short cut through Old Ma Cables orchard, never coming out of it, without at least a half dozen apples bulging in his trouser pockets each time, he had just snorted at her.

At the time, Flo's favourite programme was on and she was trying to watch it, so she wasn't best pleased with him.

'I suppose you can't expect them to be well behaved? What do you expect having a father like the one they have?' He shouted at her.

In the end to shut him up, she'd snapped back at him.

'Had, Bert, had. You know he upped and left them six months ago, and since then Becky's not heard a word from him. And, yes you're right, he wasn't a good man. The amount of times we heard him shouting at Becky and the boys, he did them a favour in moving out.' She cried out, shaking her head at him. 'Don't you think she's got enough on her plate at the moment. She has to cope all alone with them. Can't you just give her a break? She's doing the best she can.' She'd growled, as she saw the credits starting to roll, signalling the end of her programme.

She was brought back to the present, as just at that moment, Bert came to the back door and stood there stamping his feet on the wire mat, before using the boot remover to take his wellies off. Then he stepped into the kitchen in just his stocking feet. He made his way over to the sink and washed his hands, before taking Flo's clean tea towel and wiping his hands all over it. She looked at him and shook her head. It wasn't worth saying anything the mood he was in.

'They've only gone and taken two of my prize winning carrots. I was going to enter them in the village fete in a couple of weeks' time.' He said furiously.

'How do you know it's them, and not the wild rabbits that have been at them?' She snapped.

'I just do that's all.' He said looking about the kitchen for his cup of tea.

It was eleven o'clock and his tea time, which he always had with a couple of chocolate digestives. Bert was a man of routine, and did most things to time, each and every day.

'Sit down, Bert, I've made the tea, all I've got to do is pour it out.' She said shooing him away from her once clean sink.

'What I want to know?' Bert said with a mouthful of biscuit, 'is why they can't go to the supermarket like everyone else to get their veg? Why take mine?'

Flo shot him a look that said it all. He'd changed so much in the last eighteen months. He was always so moody these days. Suddenly, they were interrupted by the doorbell. Bert looked at her and Flo knew she was the one who had to go and answer it. She had the tea pot in her hands and banged it down on the kitchen table, as some of it slopped out of the spout. She turned and walked out of the kitchen, down their narrow hallway to answer it.

When she opened it up, Flo was surprised, because standing there was Becky with Fergus and Johnny.

Flo smiled tentatively at them. 'Hello, my dear? Boys, what can I do for you?'

Becky returned Flo's smile and said, 'actually I was hoping to have a word with your husband. Is he in?'

At that, Bert came out of the kitchen on hearing his name and that he was wanted. When he saw who it was at the door, he scowled at the boys, as they in turn ran and hid behind their mum's back.

'Mr Winters, I've brought the boys here to apologise to you. I've just been outside to the shed today and made a discovery.' She said, turning around and frowning at the boys.

'Go on boys, what do you have to say to Mr Winters?' She prompted them.

'We're sorry, Mr Winters, for stealing your veg and for breaking the glass in your greenhouse.' Two little voices piped up.

Becky then spoke, 'I'm sorry Mr Winters, but I just don't have the spare cash to pay for the replacement panes of glass the boys broke in your greenhouse the other week,' she said, taking a deep breath, before continuing,' but to make it up to you, the boys would like to help you out in your garden, doing whatever you want them to do to make amends. Any weeding, or cutting of your grass, then they will do it. Don't you worry on that score; they will work for you until they have paid their debt off in full.' She attempted to smile at him, but all the while he continued scowling at her and the boys.

Flo looked at the boys and could tell that they were really were truly sorry. Their faces were tear streaked. And, because she was so inquisitive, Flo was intrigued to hear what the discovery was that Becky had made in the shed. Before Bert could put his five penny worth in, she spoke and beat him to it.

'So just what did you find in the shed then, Becky?' She said, smiling at her.

Becky looked at the boys and couldn't help smiling, despite herself.

'Well the reason the boys broke the two panes of glass Mr Winters was because…there was a rabbit in there. When you came out a few weeks ago, you locked the door behind you and it was caught in there. It was trapped and desperately trying to get out. But, instead of the boys coming and telling me, so that I could come and tell you, they decided to get it out themselves, which they did by breaking the glass. And then, instead of letting it go, they decided to keep it. What they didn't realise was, the rabbit was a she…and she was pregnant, and now *she's* had six babies, all of which survived.' She shook her head looking at the boys.

'Somehow they found a big old wooden box, which they converted into a hutch; luckily it's been big enough for all of them. But now the time's right for them to be released, obviously we need to be able to take them back into the countryside and release them there. After all they are wild animals, and the boys haven't picked them up, they've been sensible there.' She smiled, suddenly looking relieved.

Flo couldn't help smiling either. *So that's who the carrots were for?* She turned around and looked at Bert and couldn't believe it! He was actually smiling too.

'Well you're going to need a lift to release those bunnies somewhere.' He said, suddenly bending down and talking, not shouting for once at the boys, 'what about me taking you both in my van?' as they nodded their small heads up and down at him in surprise.

'How old do you reckon they are now?'

'About six weeks. That's when me and Fergus got the mum out of your greenhouse. Do you think they're old enough to be let lose now?' Johnny asked wide eyed, all the while looking at Bert.

Bert nodded and said, 'I think they probably are. I tell you what? Can I come and have a look in your shed? And then we'll get our thinking caps on and find a way of getting them out of that shed and into my van.' He smiled at the boys, as once again they nodded back at him.

And then he surprised Flo by saying, 'I think that's a splendid idea your mum had about you two coming and giving me a hand in the garden. Because do you know what?'

At that, both boys shook their head.

'Well I was thinking how grand it would be to be able to show you how to grow your own vegetables. Then perhaps next year, you might be able to enter them into the local show in the village. Would you like to do that?

At that, the boys turned to their mum.

'Could we do that mum? Could we grow our own vegetables in our garden?' They asked excitedly.

'Well, we don't want to burden Mr Winters; you've both got to work your debt off…'

But, before she could say another word, Bert beat her

to it.

It would be my pleasure to be able to teach the boys about gardening. Growing your own is the best thing you can possibly do. There's nothing like eating something that you've actually grown. And I would really like to do that with your boys, if that's alright?' He asked her.

She nodded at him.

'Well if you're sure, and they won't get in your way, that would be really great.' She said smiling back.

'Are you ready to show me these here rabbits then?' He said to the boys as they excitedly nodded again.

He turned back around and put his shoes on, before grabbing his coat and cap off the hook.

'Right then, lead the way?' He said to the boys as he followed them back round to their garden.

'Becky, if you haven't got to rush off, would you like to join me in a cup of tea?' Flo asked.

'Well if you're sure, that would be lovely.' She smiled as Flo held the door wide open for her to enter.

Becky followed Flo back down the narrow corridor and through to the kitchen.

'Please take a seat, while I pour out the tea.' Flo said indicating to the chairs around the table, 'and help yourself to a biscuit too.' She said smiling at her.

'I think I owe you an explanation as to why my Bert has been so grumpy with you and your boys?'

'Oh no, you don't owe me any explanations, my boys…'

'Yes, I do. Your boys were just being boys. What you probably didn't know was that we too had a son!'

At that, Becky looked astonished.

'Although Christopher was an adult, it wasn't right that he died before us, and all because of the weather.

You see, Christopher had been driving his car in the snow, when it skidded, before crashing into a tree. He died instantly. That was almost two years ago.' Flo said dabbing her eyes with a tissue. 'That happened just before you moved in next door.'

'I'm so sorry to hear that.' Becky said putting her hand on top of Flo's as she gave her a small smile.

Flo returned her smile and said, 'I think the time has now come for a new beginning for all of us. Your boys might be just what Bert needs, to make him become that person he was, before Christopher died. Hopefully they'll give him that zest for life again.' She said as she poured the tea out, and picked up her cup, clinking it against Becky's.

20
THE EMBERS OF THE DAY
Rosemary J. Kind

"Stop fussing Freda. Let the boy come in." Papa lay back against the pillows wheezing, his skin looked paper thin, his frail hand reaching across the bedspread, quilted by his wife all those years ago. He remembered its many blue and white pieces and the hours it took her to stitch it, in the early years of their marriage. The breeze from the open window was a welcome sensation across his face.

"But you heard what the doctor said Papa, you need to rest." Freda tidied the covers of her father's bed and took his hand. It was hard to see her father like this; he had been such a strong support for her over the last few years. Even since the old man's eyesight had failed, he hadn't stopped taking care of the family.

Papa turned towards her and taking her hand in both of his said, "Freda, my time has come, we both know that rest isn't going to make any difference. Let the boy come. Let him brighten the final hours of an old man's life." Papa was prepared for what lay ahead. The thought of death didn't frighten him. He was tired. He would be reunited with Anya, but he feared for those he left behind.

Freda knew there was no point in arguing, in truth, her father was right, but she didn't want to believe that the end was so close.

The late spring sun beat down on the farmland that stretched around the house on all sides. She could see men working in the distance. The farm was never idle, Freda thought, as she went out to call her son. This was a lovely time of year in northern Italy and even now, the intensity of the light accentuated the range of colours around the courtyard; the brown stone, the green leaves, and the bright flowers in tubs by the doors.

"Pedro" Freda called, "Pedro."

The innocent brown eyes poked out from around the stable door, "Mama," Pedro replied excitedly, "the foal is standing up. Come and see."

Pedro took Freda's hand and led her into the stable. Pedro kept the stable clean and tidy, but the gentle smell of the animals hung in the air. A tiny foal struggled to remain upright on legs that wobbled awkwardly on the hay. The foal's mother stood watching protectively as Freda put her hands on Pedro's shoulders "That's wonderful darling; she's growing stronger every day." Freda hesitated, "Papa is asking for you," she said gently.

"Can I go to him?" Pedro's face lit up with excitement. He loved his grandfather. It was Papa who'd taught him to fish and to draw. It was Papa who'd brought home Snuffles. Snuffles was a scruffy little mongrel of a dog, with the sort of face that made you want to take care of it and Pedro had. It was Papa who'd sat Pedro on his knee and told him about the old times on the farm. It was Papa who'd shown Pedro how to train Snuffles to obey his every command and it was Papa who Pedro went to when he was frightened or worried. Papa had been not just a grandfather but the father he had never known. Pedro had been only six months old when his father died and his mother moved them back to live with her own father. Now he was nearly eleven and he knew that soon Papa would be gone too. He'd heard his mother talking to the doctor and although Pedro dreaded the day that Papa would be gone, he knew he had to be brave.

"Don't spend too long with him, Pedro. The doctor says he needs to rest." Even now, whatever her eyes told her, Freda didn't want to believe there was no hope.

Pedro ran across the courtyard to the house, the warm breeze giving his curly hair a tousled look, while the scents of the early summer washed over him with a quite unfounded hope. His grandfather had many dark days as his illness had progressed. There had been days when he had been too weak and in too much pain to allow Pedro to sit with him. On his good days, Pedro would sit with him and tell him everything he'd seen and all that he'd done. Sometimes he would simply sit near his grandfather and draw, describing what he drew as he went along. Pedro loved the times he could spend with the old man, even though he was now so weak. For a boy so young, Pedro had done a lot of growing up. It was hard to mourn for a father you'd never known, but he knew how much he wished his father was alive. When the other boys talked about playing football with their fathers, or told of their fathers reading to them, Pedro remained silent. He was more familiar with loss than most children of his age were, but with his grandfather's help, he learnt to carry his burden without it taking away the joy of his youth. His grandfather had taught him to honour the dead by continuing to live. To build on the legacy he had been left and savour the little pleasures in life. It was a lesson well learnt in one so young.

"Papa" said Pedro quietly as he entered his grandfather's bedroom. Pedro saw the Bible lying on the bedside table and knew it must have been his mother reading from it. A bee flew across the open window, stopping briefly but not coming in.

"Pedro" said Papa, holding out his hand. "Come child, be my eyes." The last two years since his eyesight had failed had been so hard for Papa to accept. He loved the world around him and missed seeing the changing of the seasons on the farm. "Tell me what you see."

"I saw the foal stand Papa. She's all wobbly and can't walk far without falling over, but she stood. It was amazing. Her mother is so gentle with her, but she still lets her fall over and get up on her own."

"What colour is she Pedro? What does she look like?" The hours that Papa had spent teaching Pedro to draw had paid such dividends these last two years. Papa had taught Pedro to look at the things around him properly, to see what was really there and not just to take a superficial glance at the world around him. He'd taught Pedro that to be a great artist he must see the detail, the difference between light and shade, the true lines of the world and not the corrected image that the mind presented if you didn't keep control.

"Buildings are like life," Papa would say, "they never have straight lines and perfect corners, their roofs have twists and curves, their stonework is never even."

Pedro knew how to look for the little variations that others so easily missed.

"She's the most beautiful dapple grey, with hazel eyes and the softest hair. The grey is uneven with flecks of white. When I look at her coat, I can see all sorts of patterns in the colours. It's like seeing the patterns in the flames of the fire. She's wonderful Papa."

"And at the window Pedro, what do you see?"

Pedro let go of his grandfather's hand and went over to the window.

"Tell me as though you are going to draw it Pedro. What do you see?"

"I see green shoots in the field Papa. They are waving gently in the wind. There are some places where the shoots are very small and look as though they're struggling to come through. In between the shoots, I can still see brown earth where the field was ploughed. The ploughman did well; the lines are almost straight. They are straight as a hand drawn line is straight and not as a ruler would be. The hedge is a darker green and I can see the vines on the hillside beyond. The sky is deep blue, but the colour is lighter as you look to the horizon Papa and there are no clouds anywhere. Not even the fine strands that seem so very high up and make the sky look paler. The shadow of the hedge is quite small."

"That's because it's nearly lunchtime Pedro, the sun is high."

"I know Papa," said Pedro excitedly. "You taught me how the shadows change as the sun moves across the sky. You showed me how they grow shorter and then longer again as the day goes on."

"What else can you see Pedro? Is the wisteria still out in the courtyard?"

"There are still a few flowers Papa. They look more white than purple as though the sun has faded them. Most of the flowers have died. They are brown and crumpled, dried by the sun." Pedro turned from the window towards his grandfather as though the very word of death had broken the spell of the beautiful day. "Are you going to die Papa?" Pedro asked, his voice trembling.

"Yes child, it's almost time for me to go with the wisteria. It's time for me to join the old family, time to make way for new growth. I've lived a long and happy life Pedro, it's right that I should move on."

"Why do things have to die Papa?" Pedro returned to his grandfather's bedside and his grandfather reached up to touch his tears.

"It's part of the cycle of life Pedro, the part of the plant that is old and withered must die away to make room for the new growth. Each year the wisteria grows back, beautiful new blooms on the old wood from last year. The old wood hasn't gone away, it's what gives strength to the plant, enabling it to keep growing. And so it is with people, the new generation must take their strength from the old ones. The young build on strength of the old. For two years, you have been my eyes Pedro and together we have seen many things. Now it's time for you to go on and live for me, as I can no longer do that either. Take care of your Mama, Pedro. She's going to need you to be the man of the house now child. In the same way that you have been my eyes, now you must be the eyes for your Mama."

"But Mama can see," said Pedro confused.

"Everyone can look Pedro, but not many can see. Be there to see what is real for her. Help her see light when she can only see darkness, help her to see colour when the world seems black and white. There are many ways in which we can be eyes for those we love; your Mama will need you Pedro. I am tired, I must rest now child." Papa gently touched Pedro's cheek then brought his hand down to his side on the bed. Pedro moved away towards the door, tears rolling down his face. His grandfather's message was confusing. He slipped back out to the courtyard and sat at the bottom of the wisteria looking up into its branches, Snuffles sitting beside him, nuzzling his hands. He watched the greens and pale purple seem to change their colour as the sun moved round. He watched the bees coming to the open flowers and taking pollen; he saw how they rubbed their back legs against the flowers to pick up the pollen for carrying before moving away again and others taking their place. He watched as the sun was beginning to sink lower in the sky, appearing to become a richer orange as it did so. He thought of the sunset he had drawn for his grandfather with the colours of burning embers crossing the sky. He thought too of the morning that he and Papa had woken early and gone out into the field to watch the sunrise. Beginnings and endings, endings and beginnings, a never ending wheel turning from one to the other.

He was still sitting beneath the wisteria when the shadows had lengthened and he heard his mother's crying from the window above. Pedro knew then that the time had come for his grandfather to go to the place the old wisteria flowers had gone and that it was time for him to take care of his mother. Pedro had thought a lot about his grandfather's words and he knew he must give his mother hope and comfort. Together they must see the colour that his grandfather had left behind, his legacy to both of them.

When his mother came out into the courtyard to find Pedro, he went to her and said, "Papa can see again now. The wisteria flowers are still purple where Papa is. The sky will always be blue and there will be no more darkness for him."

Freda ran her hand through Pedro's hair as she held him to her. Through her own tears, she smiled seeing how much of the old man still stood before her in the shape of her son.

Then Pedro said, "Can we take a cutting from the wisteria in the courtyard and plant it on Papa's grave, so that it will flower there every year? Purple is such a lovely colour."

21
AMANDA
Chris Cooke

I love Halloween. The seasons are changing, the air is crisp. The leaves on the trees become a myriad of iridescent colors as intense as a firework at the point of first explosion. Now I'm not what you would call the best looking man in the world so I can truly appreciate beauty like this. You see, I worked my whole life in the circus ... I was a ... well ... how do you say ... oh I'll just come out and say it ... I was a freak. That word always used to bother me until I joined up with my carnival brothers and sisters. They were the first people I had ever met that never chided me or looked away as I walked by. After about a year with them I began to be proud of the fact that I was a freak and the word itself became a source of great power for me. Being born with Proteus syndrome mixed with Gigantism, I was an eight foot tall monolithic monster. I looked like Joseph Merrick's much older and much bigger brother. Until I joined the circus, the looks of fear and loathing took their toll on my younger years but while in the circus, those same looks turned to wonder and amazement. I had thirty-two great and magical years traveling in the side show. I retired about two years ago and had enough money to buy a small house in a nice suburb here in Santa Fe, New Mexico.

I fell in love with the southwest when I traveled there for the first time with the sideshow. There is something magical about Santa Fe that cannot be put into words. You have to experience it for yourself and... well it's probably not for everyone but I am grateful for that as it wouldn't be as magical with lots of people around. Anyway, it's October 31st... and I had bought a lot of candy in anticipation of the kids in their costumes going door to door around the neighborhood in the traditional showing off of the scariest and most original costumes. As I looked out my window, the twilight was slowly beating down the brilliant autumn sunset and I thought what a perfect night for the children... you see... this was the first Halloween I decided to be a part of since I bought my house. The last two years I sat inside with the lights off as I was not comfortable showing my face to "regular" looking people. Let me tell you, when you are the only house that doesn't pass out treats... you get pretty good at cleaning egg off the windows!

Since I have lived here, I never went outside without a scarf wrapped around my face so as not to upset my neighbors. They were all very friendly but I knew that if they saw me in all my freakish glory, the stares and frightened parents grabbing their kids as I passed by would soon begin... Anyway, I had an epiphany earlier this year when I realized that Halloween was the perfect time for me as I could be myself and people would just think I was in a scary mask and costume. Once I realized this I couldn't wait to be a part of the one holiday where I could truly be myself.

Suddenly the doorbell rang! I jumped out of my easy chair and made for the door. My bowl of candy sat on the shelf eagerly awaiting its destiny as a dentist's best friend! I bought the best candy too, they would talk about my wares for the rest of the year! I opened the door and three children sang out in unison, "Trick or treat!"

Their costumes were magnificent! One was Dracula complete with blood dripping down his chin and the little girl was the scariest witch I had ever seen! The other looked just like Agent Mulder from the X-Files. It was quite a spiffy suit I may add! They all accepted their candy graciously and Dracula said, "Nice costume mister!"

I just smiled as they turned and continued their twilight journey. As I started to close the door another group of kids started up my walkway. I heard them saying that I had king size Kit Kat bars. They musta ran into Dracula and his gang. I smiled as I filled their bags with the sweet bounty. This group wore those cheesy store-bought costumes and one boy's glasses were fogged up as he wore them outside the stuffy mask. There was Kenny from South park, Darth Vader from Star Wars and Spider Man.

I passed out candy for a solid two hours when it started to slow down. All that was left was the echoes of happy hoots and hollers around the neighborhood as the kids were probably dealing with the inevitable sugar rush that will make tomorrow's school day full of candy hangovers.

I was sitting in my recliner watching "The Great Pumpkin Charlie Brown" feeling very happy that I could have normal interaction with other people... even if it is only one day a year. Yup, tonight I felt more like the confident Snoopy than the ostracized Charlie Brown. Then came a soft knock at the door. I thought all the trick or treating was over for the night but I rose from my chair, glad to make another child happy. I opened the door and there stood a lone little girl in what I think was a fairy princess costume. It was obviously homemade and I noticed that her wand was sagging and the tinfoil star was bent. She said nothing... just looked at me with big brown eyes... it reminded me of a deer's eyes the way they held wisdom, intent and sadness all in their almond-shaped prison. I noticed that she kept one arm behind her back as she stood there, holding the wand and her candy bag in the other.

"Don't you look pretty" I said with a gentle smile.

"Thank you she mumbled... you look very scary too sir... "

She averted her eyes as if she was ashamed of what she had said... it was as if she knew that this was the real me and saw right through my Halloween ruse.

"Would you like some candy?" I asked.

"Yes please…" She answered.

She raised one hand toward me and continued to hold the other behind her back. As I poured the candy by the fistful into the bag it suddenly dropped to the ground and candy flew everywhere as the bag split open upon impact. She quickly fell to her knees dropping her wand and started picking up the candy with one hand and wiping tears from her eyes with the other... well... that was when I noticed that she had no hand but her arm just ended at the wrist. She saw me looking and quickly dropped the candy and turned away walking off quickly with her shoulders moving up and down as she sobbed. Well, I was dumbstruck and shouted out to her, "What about your candy?"

She kept walking away.

"I'll give you another bag to carry it! Please come back!"

She stopped walking but did not turn around.

"Here see, I'll be right back with a bag for you."

I ran to my kitchen and returned to the door. She stood there wiping the tears from her eyes with her good hand and the other was hidden once again. I started to pick up all the spilled candy and she remained silent. I still don't know why I said this but it just came out.

"Did you know that people with your special gift get special candy?"

She looked quizzically at me.

"That's right... usually they show me their gift right away so that I know they are one of the special people."

"What do you mean special?" She asked.

"Why all the people with only one hand" I said.

She turned away in shame.

"You mean that nobody told you how special you are to have only one hand? Well, let me show you then!"

I asked her to come into my entryway but left the door open so no one would think that I was up to no good and ran to get the old cotton candy machine I took with me when I left the circus. Cotton candy was my favorite and all the other freaks chipped in to give it to me as a retirement present. I wheeled the machine into the entryway, plugged it in and ran to get the ingredients.

"Hang on princess, I won't be but a second!"

I came back and turned the machine on and poured the ingredients in and asked her to step up to the machine.

"Do you like cotton candy princess?" I asked.

"My name is Amanda but sometimes people call me Mandy and... yeah... I looove cotton candy."

"Well step right up and wave your arm in the machine but only reach in this far OK."

She reached up with her good hand and I told her that she had to use the other one as that was the only way that the cotton candy would work. She sheepishly raised her other hand and looked at me.

"You wouldn't lie to me would you mister?"

"Of course not Mandy."

She looked me right in the eye and asked me, "Are you wearing a mask?"

I froze where I stood. Her eyes were locked into my soul.

"No Mandy, I'm not... this is my real face."

She smiled and said OK and reached into the machine and said, "Now what?"

I was stunned... she seemed more at ease with me and was certainly not scared.

"Swirl your arm around... there you go... just like that!"

The cotton candy began to stick to her arm and form it's bulbous shape. She started to laugh and said, "This is fun!"

I was so pleased... she was radiating joy... this was not the same girl that rang my doorbell minutes ago.

"OK that's enough."

She now had a perfect pink cotton candy treat on her arm and looked at me expectantly.

"Well chow down!" I said.

She looked at me and mumbled, "Did other kids make fun of you too... "

"Yes Mandy they did... "

"What did you do about it?" She asked between bites of the sweet treat.

"Well... I joined the circus when I was old enough."

She looked past me and said, "So you ran away then... that's what I want to do too."

"Running away isn't the answer Mandy, why would you want to do that?"

"The other kids make fun of me and I don't fit in."

"Well they don't know how special you are now do they."

"WOW! Cotton candy! Can we have some mister?"

It was a late group of trick or treaters. Within seconds, Wonder Woman, Freddie Kruger and another Spider Man stood in my doorway.

"Hey look it's Handy!" Wonder Woman said.

"You mean Nohanda!" Freddie yelled.

They all laughed and Mandy looked toward the ground and her arm with the cotton candy quickly went behind her back. I was so mad... these were obviously some of the kids responsible for Mandy wanting to run away.

"Can we have cotton candy too mister?"

I took a step forward and said, "Do any of you have the gift?"

They looked at each other and Spider Man said, "The gift... what are you talking about sir?"

"You know, the gift... one hand... oh... I see you three are all two handers. Well no cotton candy for two handers but I do have other candy for you."

"But we want cotton candy!" They cried.

"Sorry that's just the way it is."

"But that's not fair." Pleaded Freddie Kruger.

"Maybe so but that's the way it is... now do you want candy or not?"

"You suck" said Spidey.

"C'mon let's go!" Yelled Freddie.

"Hey mister, your mask sucks too!" Chided Wonder Woman.

I knew that I would be cleaning egg off the window in the morning but I was glad to put them in their place. I turned to Amanda and she still had her hand behind her back with the cotton candy pointed down at the pavement. I looked her in the eye and told her that she was special and to never let anyone tell her differently because she was destined for great things in life and to never give up... ever.

"You better eat your cotton candy Mandy" I said.

She pulled her arm around and started in on the treat."Mmmm... it's good" She said between mouthfuls. She was smiling again.

"You best get home before your parents worry."

"Thanks sir."

"Call me Ben OK Mandy."

"Bye Ben... thanks."

She turned and walked away. I watched her as she disappeared down the street tearing pieces off the cotton candy as she walked. I closed my door and turned the cotton candy machine off. I sat back down in my chair and that's when I heard the *Pap pap pap* of eggs hitting my window. I knew who it was but I didn't care. I had made someone happy tonight and feel special and she didn't even care that I was a disfigured freak. I fell asleep to that thought.

I awoke to the sunlight and a squeaking sound... I had fallen asleep in my recliner by the fireplace. I rubbed the sleep from my eyes and looked at my front window. Amanda smiled a big smile and waved as she cleaned the egg off the window. I went outside.

"Good morning Ben! I knew this would happen so I thought I would help you out. See, I can do the cotton candy with my special arm and clean the window with this one!"

She held up both arms proudly and stood up to face me.

"I will never be ashamed of who I am again... thanks Ben."

"So no more running away huh?"

"Nope! You know what I'm gonna do Ben?"

"No, what?"

"I'm gonna clean windows until I have enough money to buy an easel and paint and then I am going to be a famous painter!"

"Well that sounds just fine Mandy. How much for my window?"

"This is for free but next time I gotta charge ya... but you will always get a discount Ben!"

I'll be damned if Amanda didn't become the premier window washer in the neighborhood. She always gave me a discount and she showed me her brand-new easel and paint set when she bought it. Her art progressed quickly and she always shared it with me... I was so proud.

The years rolled by and Mandy always got cotton candy on Halloween... and other days of the year cuz I'm a big softy. All too soon it was time for her to leave and pursue her dreams.

Well... it's been about 10 years now since she left for New York and the big shot art school that she got a scholarship to. She used to write often but I haven't heard much in the last three years or so... that's OK cuz I just know she is doing well and very happy. It's funny how one moment in time... one brief encounter can change your life or someone else's for the better... or worse... fortunately I was happy with the way I handled myself in this life...

One Sunday morning I awoke to the doorbell. I stood up, grabbed my scarf and wrapped my face. I opened the door there stood Amanda! Next to her stood a small girl about three years old and a man who I assumed to be her boyfriend or husband. Mandy grabbed the scarf and before I could do anything, she had pulled off the covering and my disfigured face was exposed... neither the girl nor the man looked away at the sight of my face... in fact they both smiled warmly.

"Hi Ben! I told you I wouldn't let you wear that damn scarf around me!"

She threw her arms around me and hugged me tightly. She stepped back and proceeded to introduce me to her husband, John and daughter Cynthia. We talked about old times and she apologized for not keeping in touch better. I told her I understood and was very happy and proud of her accomplishments.

"I have a surprise for you Ben... it's a painting I did... it's my favorite ever... I want you to have it!"

Her husband went out to their car and returned with a picture wrapped in brown canvas. He handed it to Mandy and she pulled back the canvas to reveal a painting of a small child dressed like a shabby princess and a stunningly handsome man in a prince's outfit. It was set in the marketplace of a great castle and they were standing in front of a wooden cart that said Cotton Candy in calligraphy style writing. The prince was handing the child some cotton candy and she was beaming with anticipation. The sky was a stunning blue and sunbeams made their way into the courtyard and fell upon the prince and princess.

"Wow, that's beautiful Mandy... I figure that the princess is you and I know you love cotton candy but what's with the prince?"

"Why that's you silly."

"Me... oh... but he is handsome and... perfect... and

beautiful... "

She hugged me and said quietly, "As are you Ben... you are the most beautiful person I have ever known... thank you for giving me life... "

That picture still hangs above my fireplace and I look at with love and fondness every single day. I'd be lying if I said it didn't bring a tear to my eye every single day. Amanda still keeps in touch every now and then but life goes on you know. I always wished that I could be someone who could change lives by being a dashing super hero or a handsome actor but you know what, I changed one life for the better and taught tolerance and acceptance ... you know what... that's enough. If we all did that... there would be no need for a freak show.

AUTHORS

Jan Baynham - is an enthusiastic member of two writing groups where she has been writing for her own enjoyment. She has also self-published a children's novel to share with friends and family but it wasn't until she joined a university writing class taught by a published author that she began to submit short stories for publication for a wider audience. Eventually, she would like to publish a themed anthology of short stories.

Kate Blackadder - has had almost 30 stories published in women's magazines and anthologies including New Writing Scotland. She was shortlisted for the Scotsman/Orange Short Story Award in 2006. In September 2011 she had a 7-part serial published in The People's Friend called The Family at Farrshore; Ulverscroft are bringing out a large-print edition soon.

Angela K Blackburn - enrolled on a writers' course in March 2012 which sparked her new career and from that she has been long listed in several short story competitions. She loves writing fiction, anything from 100 words to novel length in fantasy, SF, horror and romance genres. She lives in South Norfolk with her husband and a large menagerie of animals. See
http://thewritingriderblog.blogspot.co.uk

Patsy Collins - lives on the south coast of England. Her short stories regularly appear in magazines such as Ireland's Own, Woman's Weekly, That's Life! and Take a Break's Fiction Feast. Patsy's debut novel 'Escape to the Country' was published in 2012. When she's not writing, Patsy enjoys gardening, photography and travelling with her husband in their campervan. To learn more about

Patsy and her writing please visit www.patsy-collins.blogspot.com .

Caroline Scott Collins - lives on the western edge of Dartmoor. She loves travelling, and meeting new people, especially to sunny, soft white sand, palm-tree fringed locations and experiencing different cultures. Travelling fuels her imagination. She is married, has two adult sons and a new grandson. After several different careers, Caroline now works freelance. She enjoys the flexibility and freedom this allows to pursue her writing. With growing confidence to send her writing out into the world, she is working on a manuscript for her first novel A Charming Bequest. For more information read her blog – MoorScribbles

Chris Cooke - has been writing as an Author, Poet and Lyricist for twenty-seven years. He has two self-published books, The Ride and Stories For Those Of Us With A Short Attention Span. Chris also has three CD's of original music available. The newest CD, Blue Marble Symphony features a duet with the legendary Delaney Bramlett. When not writing or touring the world with various bands, Chris enjoys surfing, stunt kite flying and online gaming. www.chriscooke.net

Judith Bruton - PhD, artist/writer, moved to the Summerland Coast, New South Wales from Adelaide, South Australia in 2012. Her stories/poems are published in anthologies and online ~ alfiedog.com, ABC Open, narratorAUSTRALIA; Short and Twisted 2011, 2012, 2013; Relay, Marion Writers Inc 2011; Avant New Writing 2009. Shortlisted, Alan Marshall Short Story Award 2010. Visit: www.judithbruton.com

Tina K. Burton - has been writing short stories and articles for seven years. She has had work in publications including The Weekly News, Modern Marriages, The Lady, Real People, Twisted Tongue, and Australia's That's Life magazine. Her first novel has been signed to Crooked Cat Publishing. She is currently writing another two novels, 'Pieces of Cake', and 'Born to Love Me', a cloning based thriller. When she's not writing, she enjoys going for long walks on Dartmoor where she lives with her family.

Patricia Fawcett - has been writing for 25 years and has had one children's book published and 3 novellas before she began writing romantic fiction. Her stories are based around family life and are set both in the North of England and latterly the South West. She has had 14 novels published and her new novel 'A Small Fortune' is due out in July.

Derek Haycock - is a novelist and short story writer living in north Suffolk. Before he turned to creative writing, his career had been in research and development, mostly undertaken within multinational companies. His first novel (The Brilliance of Matt White) is available as an eBook through Amazon. He is close to finishing a second novel and has the opening and plot for a third. The only common element is that his novels are inhabited by unusual characters, upon whom life's problems fall a little harder — and a lot weirder — than for most of us, fortunately.

Suzie Hindmarsh-Knights -In her formative years Suzie Hindmarsh-Knights worked on a racehorse property in rural Victoria, gaining an in depth knowledge of the Australian racing industry. She lived in Hong Kong for five years, travelled through North and South America, Europe and Asia as well as remote trips through the Australian Outback. These experiences bring a distinctive perspective to her writing.

www.suziehindmarshknights.com

Maggie Jones - Maggie Jones lives on the beautiful Isle of Wight, where she finds the inspiration to write. Her genres are romance, comedy and drama. Bessie's Rescue is her first experience of being published with Alfie Dog, and hopes that more stories will follow suit. Maggie is chairperson of a local writing group, The Wight Fair Writers. They hold two competitions every year, encouraging people of all ages to write. All revenue from the competitions goes to support local Charities.

Susan Jones - Susan lives in Warwickshire, where she enjoys going to the gym, swimming and gardening, when she's not writing. Opening chapters of her novel, 'Hats off to Love' came on the shortlist of the Romatic Novelists New Talent Awards for 2012. You can find her website here www.susanjanejones.com She is blogging here

www.susanjanejones.wordpress.com

Rosemary J. Kind - turned to writing after a 20 year business career, although she has written as a hobby for many years. Initially she focussed on non-fiction. Her main passion, however, is fiction. She also writes her dog's daily diary as an internet blog www.alfiedog.me.uk She has won a number of prizes and short listings for her poetry and short stories. Her main hobby is developing the Entlebucher Mountain Dog breed within the UK. She has published 6 books including both fiction and non-

fiction. You can find her own writing blog at
www.rjkind.co.uk

Gill McKinlay - writes (mainly) humorous short stories and articles and has had 75 published in various magazines including Cat World, Your Cat, Woman's Weekly, My Weekly, The Weekly News, Take a Break, Fiction Feast and That's Life! (Australia).

Patricia Maw - has been writing and selling short stories for the woman's magazine market for several years. She has also sold to Scandinavia, South Africa and Australia. She did a WEA course in Creative Writing in Leicester before moving to Devon 25 years ago. Now retired she has just sold her first novel 'No More Secrets' published by AudioGo in Large Print and also available on Amazon.

Alice Parrant - has had short stories published in both Woman's Weekly Magazine and in the small press. She has also had work placed and shortlisted in a few competitions including the Yorkshire Ridings True Romance Contest. Alice tends to work best in cafes, so has developed a rather unfortunate taste for multiple cups of coffee and plates of cake! She blogs at
http://aliceinwritingland.wordpress.com

Lilliana Rose - grew up on a farm in Australia, played with DNA, taught science, and travelled, which has fed her imagination and spurred her to write. Creating Wings (2012) is her first collection of poetry. She has a Masters in creative writing at Adelaide University. Check out more of her work at: www.lillianarose.com

Annette Siketa- born in England, Annette's writing history was unremarkable until March 2008, when a routine eye operation rendered her totally blind. Her life changed completely, and it was her penchant for crafting stories that 'saved' her, although at the time, she knew nothing about professional writing. From a technical standpoint, her first novel, The Dolls House, was an unmitigated disaster. However, she persevered, and has now written numerous multi-award winning novels and short stories, covering a range of topics from children's fantasy to historical fiction.

Jeff Williams – teaches mathematics at Brandon University on the Canadian Prairies. He has written a wartime spy thriller, with another on the back burner, and he blogs about the period and setting:
http://secondbysecondworldwar.com . He co-wrote a TV screenplay based loosely on Shakespeare's Macbeth, but relocated to an orbiting space station, a thousand years from now—which is a far cry from the early-twentieth-century house where he lives with his wife and would-be-dog of a Maine Coon cat.
http://www.jeffwilliamswriter.com

Susan Wright - has had over a hundred stories published in women's magazines over the years including Take A Break's Fiction Feast, My Weekly, Chat, Yours and The Weekly News. She has also sold to magazines in Norway and Australia.

Also from Alfie Dog Fiction

This Land is My Land
16 stories for Lazy Days

Essence of Humour
17 stories to make you smile

Six Stupid Sheep and Other Yarns
13 short stories from Susan Wright

3am and Wide Awake
25 thrillers and chillers by Sarah England

Up the Garden Path
24 short stories by Patsy Collins

Home Sweet Home
12 stories children by Joan Zambelli

Double Take
A cosy crime novel by Annette Siketa

The Appearance of Truth
A novel by Rosemary J. Kind

The Sound of Pirates
An adventure novel from Terence Brand

Alfie Dog Fiction

Taking your imagination for a walk

www.alfiedog.com

Join us on Facebook
http://www.facebook.com/AlfieDogLimited

Printed in Great Britain
by Amazon

18915861R00108